20,000 LEAGUES
UNDER THE SEA

20,000 LEAGUES UNDER THE SEA

Jules Verne

Om
KIDZ
An imprint of Om Books International

First published in 2017

Om
KIDZ
An imprint of Om Books International

Corporate & Editorial Office
A-12, Sector 64, Noida 201 301
Uttar Pradesh, India
Phone: +91 120 477 4100
Email: editorial@ombooks.com
Website: www.ombooksinternational.com

Sales Office
107, Ansari Road, Darya Ganj,
New Delhi 110 002, India
Phone: +91 11 4000 9000
Fax: +91 11 2327 8091
Email: sales@ombooks.com
Website: www.ombooks.com

Adapted by Swayam Ganguly

ISBN: 978-93-84225-40-7

Printed in India

10 9 8 7 6 5 4 3 2 1

Contents

Chapter One

Strange Rumours

The year 1866 was marked by a mysterious series of incidents. A large number of ships had encountered a particular object — endlessly long, shaped like a spindle and much larger and faster than even the biggest whale. It was even reported to glow!

The ships had described the strange object in their log-books. They agreed upon all its features — its oblong shape, swift movements, surprising power and life-like energy. The length was debated — some said that it was 200 feet long, while others said it was a mile wide and three miles long. It is safe to conclude that

this sea monster was bigger than anything we had known to exist.

Owing to lack of information, talk of the subject began to die down towards the end of the year. Then, in early 1867, two accidents occurred that revived the interest.

On March 5, 1867, a ship called the *Moravian* was struck so forcefully, that its keel shattered into pieces. The sailors found nothing. All they could see was a small whirlpool-like formation around 15 feet away. But, had it not been for the ship's strong hull, she would have surely sunk.

The next accident occurred three weeks later, on April 13, when the *Scotia* was struck in the hull. But instead of being hit by a large and blunt object, this ship seemed to be pierced by something sharp. Thankfully, the damage was not enough to sink the ship.

The urgency of the situation was only realised when the ship was placed in a dry dock. The hole in the hull was a perfect isosceles triangle!

Further examination showed that it was pierced by something extremely strong, which then withdrew itself using a backward motion.

People began blaming the sea creature for all mysterious, unexplained shipwrecks. And there were quite a number of these — around two hundred per year!

I am the narrator of this story. I had a huge part to play in the story of this sea creature, as you will come to realise as I tell you more about it.

In the middle of all that fervour, I had just completed a six-month expedition studying the badlands of Nebraska in the United States of America. I was recruited for this trip by the French government, as I was an Assistant Professor at the Paris Museum of Natural History. I was to be in New York until the end of May, studying the rich specimens I had found.

Even though I was away from home, I knew of all that was occurring in the sea. How could I not? It was all that every American and

European newspaper worth its salt could talk of. I had read the reports and still could not find a way to explain the mystery.

"Could it be a floating island?" I wondered. But floating islands do not move so quickly.

"Perhaps it is the floating hull of a wrecked ship," I tried. "No—those cannot move very quickly either."

I realised that there were only two possibilities—either it was a colossal sea monster or an underwater ship.

How could a person build such a technologically advanced project? It would have to be built by a government. But governments would find it impossible to build such a huge vessel in secret. There would be too much interference from rival governments.

Soon, people far and near began formally asking for my opinion on the matter. While in France, I had published a book titled *The Mysteries of the Great Ocean Depths*, which

was well-received by the critics. It promptly established me as an expert in this rather obscure field of natural history.

So, I was invited to publish an article detailing my opinions on this matter by *The New York Herald*. This is roughly what I wrote:

There are two assumptions we can make — either we know of all the animals that exist, or we do not.

If we do not know about all the animals in existence, then it is very likely that a large, powerful cetacean has found its way to shallow waters by accident.

If, on the other hand, we do know about all the animals, then we must look for the mysterious animal from amongst those that we already know of. Thus, I am inclined to accept the existence of a giant narwhal.

The common narwhal — also called the sea-unicorn — reaches a length of sixty feet. Increase its size and power by five or ten times, and you will have the animal that we seek. This giant narwhal is

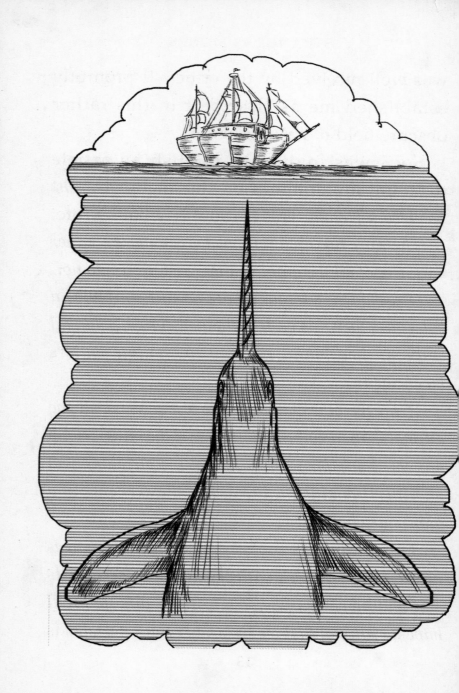

equipped with a single tusk or halberd, which is as hard as steel. They have been found buried inside the bodies of whales. Its tusk, no longer a mere lance, would be as strong as the spur of a battleship or a ram of war — strong enough to pierce the hull of the Scotia.

My article was a success! The human mind takes great delight in imagining fantastic creatures. But some people choose to look at the more practical side of things. These people were more concerned with capturing the sea monster and making the oceans safe once again.

The United States decided to take initiative and capture the dangerous creature. They prepared a high-speed frigate called the *Abraham Lincoln* and appointed the erstwhile Commander Farragut to lead the chase.

The ship was equipped with the finest equipment and technology. The crew was appointed and the ship was stocked with supplies. However, when all the preparations were made, the monster seemed to have disappeared entirely! It had not been sighted by any ship for a very long time.

On July 2, they received news that the creature had been spotted in the North Pacific Ocean. Just three hours before the *Abraham Lincoln* was to depart, I received the following letter:

Sir,

If you would like to join in the expedition on the Abraham Lincoln, *the government of the United States will consider you as France's representative. Commander Farragut has reserved a cabin for you.*

Cordially,

J.B. Hobsen,

Secretary of the Navy

Three seconds after I had read it, I felt as though hunting this creature down was the purpose of my life.

"Conseil!" I called out to my manservant. He was a pleasant, devoted Flemish lad who joined me on all my missions. Conseil was quiet, hardworking, good at his work and despite having a name that means 'counsel', he never offered advice — even when asked for it!

He was thirty years old while I was forty! Conseil had one flaw — he was a stickler for formality and he would only speak to me in third person.

"Conseil!" I repeated.

I had never bothered to consult him before leaving on any trip. But this one was going to be dangerous and indefinitely long.

"Conseil!"

This time, Conseil appeared. "Did master call for me?" he asked.

"Yes," I replied. "Get our bags ready. Pack my travelling kit and as many clothes as you can. We leave in two hours."

"What about master's fossil collection?" asked Conseil.

"We will have the hotel send it to Paris for us," I said.

Sir,

If you would like to join in the expedition on the Abraham Lincoln, the government of the United States will consider you as France's representative. Commander Farragut has reserved a cabin for you.

Cordially,
J. B. Hobson,
Secretary of the Navy

"We are not going back to Paris, then?" asked Conseil.

"Oh … we are, certainly," I said cautiously. "But we are making a slight detour. We are leaving on the *Abraham Lincoln* to look for the giant narwhal," I said. "A glorious mission, but a dangerous one! I do not want to deceive you, so think it over. This is the kind of mission that men do not always return from."

But Conseil did not bat an eyelid. "Where master goes, I go," he said.

Ever diligent, he immediately set about packing our luggage and arranging for transportation. In no time at all, we found ourselves on board the *Abraham Lincoln*, face-to-face with a smart-looking officer. "Professor Pierre Arronax?" he asked me.

"The one and only! Commander Farragut?"

"In the flesh," he said. "Welcome aboard. Your cabin awaits you."

The *Abraham Lincoln* was a fine frigate, equipped with superheating chambers that would give it considerable average speed — 18.3 nautical miles an hour. I was happy with my cabin, too. "We'll be quite comfortable here," I said to Conseil.

I left Conseil to stow the suitcases away while I climbed out on the deck. I could see Commander Farragut ordering the last anchors to be loosened. If I had arrived even fifteen minutes later than I had, the *Abraham Lincoln* would have sailed without me! I would not have had the extraordinary adventure that I am about to narrate to you — even though you may not believe it's true.

"Are we on full steam?" I heard Commander Farragut ask one of his crewmen.

"Yes, sir," replied the man.

"Let's go ahead!" cried Commander Farragut.

Chapter Two

Aboard the *Abraham Lincoln*

Commander Farragut was a good sailor who matched his vessel well. In fact, it could be said that the vessel and the sailor were not two different entities, but one being. The *Abraham Lincoln* was the body and he was its soul.

He had no doubt that the narwhal existed. He believed in its existence as certain religious people believe in the leviathan — not by having seen it, but by faith. Either Commander Farragut would kill the narwhal or it would kill him. There was simply no other alternative.

The sailors on board shared the belief of their commander. They were constantly

discussing the means by which they would catch the monster while watching the sea with rapt attention. Our ship had good reason to be renamed *Argus*, after the mythical beast with a hundred eyes!

The *Abraham Lincoln* was loaded with the finest, most advanced weapons that a hunting ship could need. But it also had Ned Land, the King of Harpooners.

Ned Land was Canadian, but known all over the world. His skill with the harpoon was a rare and special gift. He was my age, over 6 feet tall, strong, brooding and ill-tempered when trifled with. He had an intense gaze that gave him a distinguished look.

Ned Land was generally aloof but he took a liking to me. He would enthral me with tales of his adventures in the polar seas. His style of narration was naturally lyrical—I felt as though I was listening to a Canadian Homer reciting the *Iliad* of the Arctic regions!

Ned was the only member of the crew who did not believe in the sea-unicorn. He avoided talking about the matter completely. However, I wasn't about to let it go so easily.

"Why do you not believe in the monster?" I asked. "A whaler like you ought to be the most excited about it!"

"That's where you're mistaken, Professor!" replied Ned. "The common man may believe in such rumours, but as someone who has seen, caught and slain several sea mammals, I know better."

"And what about the giant narwhal is so unbelievable?" I questioned.

"Well, everything!" scoffed Ned. "But what cements my disbelief is this—I have never encountered an animal with a tail or halberd strong enough to even scratch the iron hull of a ship."

"You are forgetting that this creature resides in the far depths of the ocean," I argued.

"This means that it possesses strength beyond anything we have seen before."

"And why is that so?" asked Ned, his tone full of disbelief.

"Because it takes great strength to be able to live so deep underwater!" I replied. "Let me explain. We are surrounded by a thick blanket of air. At every moment, the air around us is putting pressure on each of us. This pressure is very great – more than 17,000 kilograms!"

"How does the body withstand this pressure?" inquired Ned. "I hardly feel anything!"

"This is because the air inside our bodies exerts an equal pressure," I explained, encouraged by his interest. "This helps us maintain a balance. If it was not for our internal pressure, we would be flatted by the air."

"What does this have to do with the sea monster?"

"You see," I replied, "deep under the water, creatures have to withstand the pressure

27

from all the water above them. This pressure is equal to a thousand times more than air pressure. If you or I dove that deep, we would be trampled flat!"

"Fire and brimstone!" Ned interjected.

I chucked, "If a huge animal with a heavy structure can support itself at such depths, can you imagine its strength?"

"Why, it would have to be as strong as an armoured frigate, with flesh as strong and thick as eight-inch steel plating!" said the Canadian.

"Then why do you find it so hard to believe that such a creature can pierce through the hull of a ship?" I cried victoriously.

But Ned was not willing to give in. "Yes ... indeed ... maybe ...," he dawdled. "But it just couldn't be true!"

This reply proved nothing except the extent of Ned's stubbornness. But to find out more, the creature would need to be dissected. To be dissected, it would first have to be caught, which was Ned Land's business. To be caught, it would first have to be sighted, which was the crew's business. To be sighted, it would first have to be encountered — which was a risky and uncertain business.

By July 6, the *Abraham Lincoln* entered the Pacific Ocean, where the monster had last been sighted. "Keep your eyes wide open!" reminded the sailors. And keep them wide open we did. I ate for only a few minutes and slept for only a few hours each day.

If, by chance, we spotted a whale, the whole crew would crowd onto the deck, our eyes peeled. We would chase the cetacean, only to find it was a regular whale that would soon disappear under the waves.

As the months flew by, it was the most passionate sailors who became the ones who were most convinced that the voyage was futile. Had they been in command, they would have turned the ship around a long time ago.

Finally, Commander Farragut could not ignore the crew's discontentment. "Let us give it another three days," he said. "If we do not spot the beast until noon of November 5, we will return home."

This announcement gave us a renewed sense of enthusiasm as we searched the seas once more. Two days passed without any progression. Then, on the night of November 5, as I was having a chat with Conseil, I heard Ned Land's voice pierce through the air.

"There it is!" he shouted, excited. "The thing we all seek!"

Chapter Three

The Chase

The whole ship's crew abandoned their posts and rushed to where Ned Land was standing. It was very dark, but it was plain to see that the Canadian had made no mistake. Two cable lengths away, a patch in the sea shone brightly.

"This is no natural glow," I said. "It comes from electricity. But the object is moving — it's coming towards us!"

A cry of panic rose from the ship. "Silence!" called the Commander. "Right your helm! Engines forward!" The crew immediately got to work, steering the ship away.

But as we retreated away from it, it followed us at double our speed! We could only stand and stare at the approaching patch of light. The animal started circling the ship, creating rings of light like shining dust.

It moved two or three miles away, almost fading into the horizon, gathering force. The very next minute, it charged towards us again!

We braced ourselves for the impact, but it never came. The creature stopped two feet away from us, its light going off in a flash. We saw it reappear on the other side of our ship—either by going around us or under our hull.

The *Abraham Lincoln*, was now fleeing! I brought this up with Commander Farragut. His face was stamped with astonishment.

"Professor Arronax," he said, "I do not know the strength of this creature. I refuse to put my ship in danger. We will attack in the morning, when we can see clearly."

"You have no doubts as to which creature it is?" I asked.

"None," he replied. "I am sure it is a giant, electric narwhal. And if it has the power to electrocute us, then it is the most fearsome creature ever created."

The narwhal mimicked the speed of the ship, but did not attack. At around midnight, the narwhal's light died out, as if it were a huge glow worm. Had it fled? Nobody could tell. However, less than an hour later, the crew heard a deafening whistle.

"Do whales make such a whistle?" I asked Ned Land.

"Often, sir," replied Ned, "but never this loud. Let me get close enough to harpoon it, and then I will silence it forever. At 2 o'clock in the morning, the light reappeared five miles away from us. Despite the distance and the screeching wind, we could still hear the creature thrashing its tail and breathing heavily. The moment the creature came to the surface, its lungs sucked in the air as if it were a 2,000-horsepower machine.

"Hmm," I thought. "A whale as strong as cavalry regiment!"

We prepared the ship and ourselves all night. At 6 o'clock, at daybreak, the narwhal's electric glow faded away. Alas, a thick morning mist formed around us, making it impossible to see clearly. It only cleared at 8 o'clock. This was when the *Abraham Lincoln* advanced towards the cetacean.

As I got a closer look, I realised that it was only about 250 feet in length. While I was watching, two jets of water and steam rose 40 feet into the air from its blowholes. Thus, I concluded that it was definitely a cetacean — but whether it was in the family of sperm whales, baleen whales or dolphins, I was still unsure.

A loud cry from Commander Farragut broke into my thoughts. "Fire up the furnaces!" he yelled. "Let's go full steam!"

Three loud cheers greeted this order. It was time for the battle. But the narwhal seemed

unconcerned. It was too quick for the *Abraham Lincoln* to get within even two fathoms of it. Commander Farragut was getting frustrated. "Mr Land," he said, "do you suggest that we lower the longboats and attempt to get closer?"

"No, sir," replied Ned. "We cannot catch it so easily."

"Then what do you propose?"

"Stoke up more steam, sir," said Ned. "With your permission, I will perch myself at the bowsprit. If we get close enough, I will throw my harpoon."

"Go, Ned," said the commander. "Engineer, mount the pressure!"

Ned Land went to his post. The engineer cranked up the pressure. At this rate, the *Abraham Lincoln* was moving at 18.5 miles an hour. But the animal swam away just as fast!

The chase continued all day, with the frigate reaching a top speed of 19.3 miles an hour. But the creature sped up without the slightest effort!

Commander Farragut had gone from twirling his beard to gnawing it with anxiety. "Let's fire at it!" he ordered.

The bullets hit the narwhal – and then slid off its body. On that unlucky day, we chased the narwhal for no less than 300 miles. Then, night came again.

We had all but given up, until at about 11 o'clock in the evening, when we spotted it floating motionless upon the waves. It seemed to be asleep. We advanced towards it slowly and quietly, until we reached quite close to it.

I saw Ned Land holding onto the bowsprit with one hand. With the other hand, he was brandishing his harpoon with rapt concentration. At once, his arm shot forward, launching the harpoon. It clanged loudly, as if it had hit something hard.

And then, the narwhal's light went out. Two huge spouts of water crashed into the frigate . A shocking collision came next, and I was thrown over the rail into the deep sea.

Chapter Four

Cast Away

The shock of my fall was intense. At first, I was drawn around twenty feet underwater. I had enough presence of mind to swim back to the sea surface.

There was darkness all around me. In the distance, I saw a black mass disappearing towards the east. It was the *Abraham Lincoln*!

"Help! Help!" I shouted, desperately swimming towards the frigate. Water was gushing into my mouth. "Help!" I shouted again—my last shout...

Suddenly, I felt a pair of strong arms lift me up to the surface. "If master would lean

on my shoulder, master would find it easier to swim."

"Conseil!" I gasped. "You fell off, too?"

"Not at all. But being in master's service, I followed master down."

"What about the frigate?" I asked.

"Well, just as I jumped overboard, I heard the crew shouting about the propeller being broken by the monster. Until they can get it fixed, the ship will not follow the rudder! It will simply go where the waves carry it."

This was horrible news! Our only chance was to be rescued by one of the frigate's longboats. Conseil and I had to stay afloat. We formed a system by which one would lie motionless, allowing the other to pull us forward. We took turns of ten minutes each. Only two hours later, I was overcome with exhaustion. Conseil had to bear the burden of us both, and I could hear the poor, faithful lad gasping desperately.

"Leave me! Leave me!" I said to him.

"Never!" Conseil said. "I'd sooner drown."

Poor Conseil was running out of strength, but he still managed to articulate cries of "Help! Help!" in between intervals. Then, as if in response to his calls, I heard a buzzing sound nearby.

Conseil threw another desperate cry into the air. This time, there was no mistaking it—a human voice mumbled a reply! Conseil guided us both towards the voice. Just when I was getting delirious, I banged into something hard and found myself being lifted up again. I blacked out with exhaustion, opening my eyes a while later, only to see the face of Ned Land.

"Ned!" I exclaimed. "You were thrown overboard, too?"

"Yes, Professor," he replied. "But I was luckier than you. As soon as I fell, I managed to remain afloat on this floating island—or, should I say, on our gigantic narwhal."

"Whatever do you mean?" I asked.

"You see, Professor," said Ned, "when my harpoon was blunted and couldn't puncture the narwhal, I understood that it was made of boilerplate steel."

Those words flicked a switch in my brain. I kicked the smooth black surface underneath me. It was strong and hard, not soft like flesh. This was no animal made by God, but a man-made machine!

"So this is an underwater ship," I said. "If so, it must also have a crew."

"Maybe," shrugged Ned Land. "But it hasn't shown any life for the three hours that I've been here. All it does is float upon the waves."

Just then, the machine stirred to life, rising around 80 centimetres above water. The three of us held on for dear life.

"As long as it moves above water," said Ned, "I have no complaints. But if it decides to dive, we are all done for."

This thought set us into motion. We began to bang and kick at the hull, calling out for help until our throats were sore. When daylight broke, I felt a sense of accomplishment. We had made it through the harrowing night! But then, the ship began to sink a little. We began to get really desperate.

"Ned Land kicked the metal underneath him. "Let us in, you hostile pirates!"

Fortunately, the sinking stopped. From inside the ship, we could hear the sound of heavy iron locks being undone hastily. An iron plate flew up, and in its place, a man's head emerged. He gave a shout in an odd language and immediately went down again.

A few moments later, eight men appeared. They grabbed us roughly by the shoulders and dragged us down the fearsome machine.

Chapter Five

Mobilis in Mobili

The abduction happened so quickly, that neither I nor my friends were able to collect ourselves. We were pushed down a shaft into the vessel. I found my feet clinging to the rungs of an iron ladder, with Conseil and Ned following through. As soon as we reached the bottom, we were pushed through a door which slammed shut behind us.

We were alone and surrounded by complete darkness. Ned, displeased with the proceedings so far, broke the silence. "These people are as hospitable as savages!"

"Calm down," I told Ned. "Let's try to find out where we are first." I felt the riveted boilerplate walls, a wooden table and some wooden stools. The floor was covered with some sort of thick hemp carpet, which quietened our footsteps. As I was carrying out my examination, the room suddenly filled with a blinding electric light.

When my eyes got adjusted to the light, I saw that it came from a globe carved into the ceiling. It allowed me to get a good look at the room — it was tiny, with only the table and stools as furniture.

The first man was stocky and muscular, with broad shoulders, a squat head and luxuriant, jet black hair on his head and upper lip.

The other man deserves a more detailed description. His face was an open book; it clearly showed his dominant qualities — his head was raised with self-confidence, his black eyes glazed with assurance, his pale skin gave him an air of calmness, his knitted brows showcased his pent-up energy and his vital, deep breaths showed off his courage. In his presence, I could not help but feel reassured.

Whether this stranger was thirty-five or fifty, I could not say. He was tall, with a large forehead, straight nose, a sharp mouth, pristine teeth and slender hands. His eyes were spaced farther apart than usual, which helped him see a wider range than most people. This gave him a great sense of vision—even better than Ned Land's. It seemed as though he was looking into your soul.

The two men were dressed in garments of a strange material. The fur of their caps was taken from the sea otter and their boots were sealskin. The taller man examined us closely and then turned to his companion, speaking in a strange tongue. The two of them then fixed their attention upon me.

"I do not understand what you say," I said in French. I recounted the entire story to them. They didn't seem to understand a word.

"Try speaking in English," I said to Ned Land, who once more repeated the account in his tongue. They looked at us politely while we spoke. However, they did not give us any indication that they could understand us.

Finally, Conseil recounted the story in German. This, too, had no effect on the strange men. Once again, the strangers exchanged a few words in the unknown language and left the room.

"What rudeness!" spat Ned. "We spoke to them in French, English and German, but they did not have the politeness to answer!

"Perhaps they did not understand us, Ned," I reasoned. "They certainly look as though they have foreign blood — Spanish, Turkish, Arabian or Indian. As for their language, I haven't the foggiest idea where it is from!"

"That is the disadvantage of not speaking every language," said Conseil, "or of not having one universal language!"

Just then, the door opened. A steward walked in with food and fresh clothes. While we dressed ourselves, the steward set the table for us and quietly left.

The dinner that he has served was a delicious mix of seafood, but I could not identify any of its components. We ate using cutlery made of bell metal, and each plate, knife, fork and spoon had the same engraving:

The 'N' was probably the name of the captain of the ship—which, I had no doubt, was the enigmatic gentleman who we had met earlier. We devoured all the food which we had received, and then, we fell into a deep sleep.

I do not know for how long we slept, but I was the first one to wake up. I looked around the cell — nothing had changed. We were still prisoners. However, the steward had cleared up the plates while we were sleeping. Suddenly, I became aware of my laboured breaths — we were running out of air.

I became desperate for fresh air and could feel my chest tightening. Suddenly, I felt the vessel rising upwards. A moment later, my lungs were filled with fresh, salty air. Surely the vessel had surfaced for fresh air, just as other sea mammals do. I easily found the ventilator which let fresh air into the cabin.

Conseil and Ned awoke at the same time, presumably under the influence of the pure air entering their lungs. "Did master sleep well?" asked Conseil.

"Very well," I replied. "What about you, Mr Ned Land?"

"Soundly," he said. "But I am ravenous. Surely we have slept for more than 24 hours. I do hope they serve us breakfast soon."

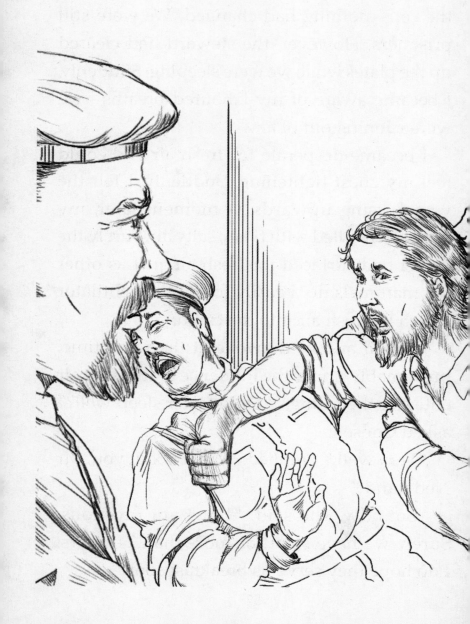

We chatted with one another for an hour or two, but there was no sign of food. Were they trying to starve us? I felt a wave of terror sweep through my body. Conseil stayed calm, whereas Ned started to get very anxious and restless. He began shouting on the top of his voice. But nobody could hear us.

After a long wait, we finally heard the sound of footsteps outside the cell. When the door opened, a steward walked through it. Ned flew towards his throat and tackled him against the wall. Conseil rushed to save the poor man, and I joined him. That's when I heard a voice speak to me in clear French: "Calm down, Mr Land! And you, Professor, kindly listen to me!"

Chapter Six

Captain Nemo

It was the ship's commander. Hearing his voice, Ned straightened up immediately. The poor steward, scrambled out of the cell at one gesture from his commander. For once, Conseil seemed excited. As for me, I was shocked!

After a few moments of silence, the commander spoke. "Gentlemen," he said. "I was only pretending not to understand you. I speak French, English, German and even Latin with equal fluency.

Having listened to your story thrice, I have come to know your identities. I now know that sheer chance has brought Professor Arronax, his

trusted manservant Conseil and the harpooner Ned Land into my presence."

I nodded in agreement. The man spoke in perfect French. Yet, he did not seem to me like a fellow countryman.

The commander continued. "I wanted some time to consider how to deal with you. You see, you have had the misfortune of coming across a man who is completely cut off from society. It's been quite an annoyance to me."

"It was by mistake," I put in.

"Was it by mistake that the *Abraham Lincoln* was trying to hunt me, with all of you on it? Or that your bullets bounced off my plates? Was it by mistake that Mr Ned Land struck me with his harpoon?"

"You have to understand that we thought you were a dangerous monster," I said.

The commander smiled wryly. "Are you telling me, Professor," he said, "that you would not have tried to hunt me, had you known that I was manning a submarine vessel?"

This question embarrassed me. Commander Farragut would probably not hesitate to attack a submarine, believing it to be his duty.

"So now you understand why I have the right to treat you like an enemy?" asked the commander. "It would be perfectly within my rights to throw you all overboard!"

"A savage might do something of that sort," I said, "but not a civilised gentleman."

"Professor," said the commander sternly. "I am not what you call a civilised gentleman. I do not obey the laws of society, and I request that you do not bring them up again!"

A flash of anger came upon the man's face, and for a moment, I got a glimpse of his terrible past. Nobody could trifle with this man. He was only answerable to his god — if he believed in one — and his conscience — if he had one.

"I have decided," said the commander, "that since fate has brought you here, you will continue to live on this ship. You will be free. But I have one condition—there may be times when I will have to lock you up in your cabins— maybe for days at a time. I do this for your own good, as you are innocent from things that you do not know about. Do you accept?"

"We do," I answered for my friends and myself. "But given the chance to return to land, will you allow us to do so?"

"I am afraid not," he replied. "You will have to be life-long members of this vessel."

This evoked a strong outcry from Ned. "I will never promise that I won't try to escape!" he said.

"I do not ask for your word," said the strange commander. "You are my prisoners. You attacked me. You have come to be aware of my secret world. I am not interested in

keeping you as prisoners. It is my secrets I am worried about."

Then, in a softer voice, he continued, "Do not worry. Professor Arronax, your book has a place in my library. You have done a good job, but there are still some things that you do not know. If you join me on my vessel, you will have a chance to do so."

It's true — the commander's words had an astounding effect on me. "Sir," I said, "we are castaways who you have been kind enough to accommodate. I speak for myself when I say that the enticement of research override my want for freedom. But I have one last question — what should I call you?"

"I go by Captain Nemo," said the formidable commander. "And you are all passengers on the *Nautilus*. Mr Land and Conseil, a meal awaits you in your cabin. The steward outside will guide you. As for you, Professor, you will breakfast with me."

Chapter Seven

The *Nautilus*

I followed Captain Nemo into an electrically-lit passageway, which led to a dining room, decorated and furnished meagrely but tastefully. The silverware shone under the light, which was softened by the paintings on the walls.

Our table stood at the centre, richly laden with food. I took a seat and helped myself. The food seemed to have been mostly — if not completely — provided by the sea. Although it was delicious, I had no idea what I was eating.

I tasted all those dishes and more while Captain Nemo regaled me with his extraordinary tales. "The sea," he said, "is everything. Life

began from the sea—who is to say it will not end in it? The sea is peace. It belongs to nobody. On its surface, men can still fight the horrors of society. But thirty feet under, they cease to reign. They have no influence here. I have made my home in the bosom of the waters. I have no masters! I am free!"

By now, I had finished my breakfast and was listening to him eagerly. "Now, Professor," he said, "allow me to take you on a brief tour of the *Nautilus*."

Once again, I followed Captain Nemo as he walked through a double-door. We entered a room as big as the one we had just exited. It was a library, filled to the ceiling with shelves lined with uniformly-bound books. There were huge leather divans and light movable desks, which made for great comfort. I was awestruck! "Captain Nemo," I exclaimed. "This library would impress me even if it were in a palace. It's a sheer miracle that it is a part of your vessel."

"Where else can one find greater solitude than in the ocean?" replied Captain Nemo.

"Rightly said, sir," I agreed. "You must have six or seven thousand volumes here!"

"Twelve thousand, Professor," said the captain. "And all of them are available to you."

I peered through the shelves. There were books on science, morals, literature, and every other subject, but not one book on political economy. Also, the books were not arranged in a specific order.

"Thank you, sir," I said. "This library contains many treasures of science that will be useful to me."

But Captain Nemo was already leading me through another door! It was a vast, splendidly-lit museum. Its ceiling was decorated with motifs and it contained various and rather mismatched treasures of nature and art.

Thirty beautiful paintings separated by bright curtains decorated the walls. I saw works of great value and of several old masters such as Raphael, Leonardo da Vinci and Titian. The modern paintings bore signatures of the likes of Delacroix, Ingres, Decamps, and others. Upon the pedestals stood some exquisite marble and bronze statues and the finest antiques I had ever seen. There were also specimens of several kinds of ocean life and instruments which were a mystery to me. It also had a piano!

It was impossible to estimate the value of this collection. I was amazed by the *Nautilus*.

"I may not know you, Captain," I said, "but one thing I do know is that you are a man of superior taste. But if I spend all my admiration on this collection, I will have none left for the vessel which carries it! It is the *Nautilus* and how it works that excites my curiosity the most."

"I will explain all this to you with great pleasure," said Captain Nemo. "But first, come have a look at your cabin." I followed him towards the bow of the ship, where I

found, not a cabin, but an elegant room. It had a comfortable bed, a dressing table and other pieces of furniture.

"Your room is joined to mine," he said, opening another door. "And my room opens to the museum."

The captain's room was extremely bare-boned — a small iron bedstead, a table and a few toiletries. It did not even have electric lights — it was lit by a circular port hole in the wall. However, there were lots of charts, graphs and other instruments all around.

"Now, if you will have a seat," said Captain Nemo, "I will explain how the *Nautilus* works." He pointed to the instruments hanging from the walls of his room. "You might be familiar with some of these — the thermometer, which tells us the temperature inside the *Nautilus*; the barometer, which indicates the air pressure and foretells changes in the weather; the hygrometer, which marks the humidity; the compass, which guides the course of the *Nautilus* ..."

"Yes, these are the usual nautical instruments," I replied. "And I know how each of them work. But some others, I am not very sure of."

"Those, Professor," he began, "will require explanation. There is a powerful force that powers everything on my vessel. It provides, light, warmth and even the power for my mechanical apparatus. This force is electricity!"

"Nothing but Electricity?" I cried in surprise. "How can a vessel that moves so fast be powered by electricity? Until now, we have only managed to use electricity in restraint to produce a small amount of power."

"Professor," said Captain Nemo, "my electricity comes from sea water, which is rich in sodium." I use this sodium to create my electricity. I get everything from the ocean — I could even manufacture air from it! But I have no need for that, because I go up to the surface as and when I want to."

The captain explained how the different instruments ran on electricity — even the 24-hour clock!

"There's even more!" said Captain Nemo. "Please join me at the stern of the *Nautilus*."

We went past all the rooms that I had just looked at. The doors were all sealed with India-rubber, so that in case of a leak, the *Nautilus* would not get completely flooded.

At the centre of the vessel, I spotted an iron ladder leading upwards. I asked Captain Nemo what the ladder led to.

"The longboat, of course!" he replied. "It's an insubmersible vessel that I use for pleasure or to go fishing."

"If it is insubmersible, then wouldn't the *Nautilus* have to go to the surface when you wished to embark on it?"

"Not at all," replied the captain. "The boat is kept bolted down in a water-tight cavity. This ladder leads me through a hole in the side of the longboat. Once I enter, I seal the hole shut

and unbolt the longboat. It rises to the surface of the sea with ease, and I take it for a spin."

"But how does it return to the submarine?" I asked.

"The submarine comes to me! An electric thread connects the longboat to the *Nautilus*. All I have to do is send a telegraph.," said Nemo

As we passed to the other half of the vessel, I saw Conseil and Ned Land's cabin, the galley, the bathroom and the crew's quarters. But, the door was shut, denying me the chance to estimate how many men were onboard.

We finally came to the engine room, where Captain Nemo had arranged his locomotive machinery. I examined it with great interest.

"With the help of these machines, I can move at a speed of fifty miles an hour."

"I don't find this hard to believe," I said. "But I have so many questions about your vessel."

"Let us go to the library, where I will answer your questions in detail."

We made ourselves comfortable on a couple of divans, and I began to ask my questions.

"How are you able to see in the dark ocean depths, where not even an ounce of sunlight can penetrate?"

"We use glass lenses that are thirty or more times thicker than the toughest quality of glass used on land. This ensures that they do not break underwater. We also have a powerful electric reflector, which can light up the ocean for half a mile in front of us."

"Ah! Bravo!" I congratulated. "That explains the phosphorescence that we thought came from the narwhal.

But now, I ask you—was the incident with the *Scotia* an accident?"

"Yes, completely," said the Captain. "As for the *Abraham Lincoln*, it was attacking me. I am sorry for the loss I caused, but I had to defend myself. Besides, I only disabled her engines—that is something they can get repaired with ease."

"How could you construct this vessel in secret?" I asked.

"That was simple," said the captain. "I simply ordered each separate part from different parts of the world — under different names!"

"But how did you manage to put together all these parts?"

"That was simple, too," he replied. "I set up my workshop on a deserted island in the middle of the ocean, where my workmen and I put together the vessel. When our work was done, we destroyed all evidence on the island."

"Surely the cost of this vessel is immense?" I inquired. "You must be extremely rich!"

"I could pay off the national debt of France without feeling the pinch," he said.

I gaped at Captain Nemo, open-mouthed. Was he lying to me? Only time could tell.

Chapter Eight

The Voyage Begins

My journey aboard the *Nautilus* began in the Pacific Ocean. Captain Nemo invited me up to the surface so that we could find out our starting point. I found myself standing on the upper hull of the *Nautilus*.

The platform we stood on was only about three feet above water. I could see the *Nautilus* in all its cigar-shaped glory. Its iron plates slightly overlapped one another, much like scales. It was plain to see why it was often mistaken for a sea animal.

It was a beautiful day. Captain Nemo measured the altitude of the sun using his

sextant. He stood so steadily, that the instrument could not have been more stable even if it was held by a hand that was made of marble.

"It's 12 o'clock, November 8," he said, "the day we begin our exploration of the waters. Now, with your permission, I will retire."

Captain Nemo bowed and left, leaving me alone with my thoughts. I went back into the vessel, where I met Conseil and Ned. They were astounded with what they saw.

"Are we in the Quebec museum?" asked the harpooner.

"It feels like the Sommerard artefacts exhibition!" exclaimed Conseil.

"My friends," I said, "you are neither in Canada, nor France, but on the *Nautilus* — deep down in the ocean!"

"How many men do you think are on board?" asked Ned, clearly with an intention to know whether planning escape or mutiny was possible.

"I don't know, Mr Land," I replied. "Besides, it is better not to entertain the idea of rebelling against Captain Nemo. This vessel is a modern masterpiece. Many people would happily trade places with us. So let us remain calm, at least for the moment, and enjoy the sights around us."

"How will we see anything at all while we remain trapped in this horrid iron prison?" asked the Canadian.

At that very moment, darkness fell upon us. We remained, paralysed with surprise. Suddenly, a sliding noise was heard. It sounded as though the panels of the *Nautilus* were moving. Just as suddenly, light broke on either side of the room, through two large windows. We could see the water for at least a mile all around, lit up by the vessel's electric gleam. What a sight to behold! What pen can describe it? Who could paint the effect of the light passing through the transparent layers of water? Or the softness of the water as it got darker with depth?

"Your pleas were answered, Ned," I said.

"How interesting!" muttered the Canadian, forgetting his frustration. "What wouldn't one do for a view like this?"

There was an army of beautiful sea creatures in every direction. Conseil and Ned made a game of identifying them.

"A triggerfish," said I, pointing towards one.

"It's a Chinese triggerfish," said Ned Land.

"Genus *Balistes*, family *Scleroderma*, order *Plectognatha* ..." Conseil chanted.

For the next few days, I spent my time reading, relaxing and chatting with my companions. I saw no sign of Captain Nemo.

On November 11, the *Nautilus* rose to the ocean's surface for oxygen. I went up the iron steps to the platform on the upper hull. I was admiring the view when I heard the sound of footsteps. I was expecting it to be Captain Nemo, but it was his second-in-command — the stocky man I had met during the captain's first visit. Ignoring me, he brought out his telescope and scanned the horizon in every direction. Then, he pronounced the following phrase:

"Nautron respoc lorni virch."

I did not know its meaning, but I heard him repeat the same words for several days to come. Still, there was no sign of Captain Nemo.

On November 16, when I was starting to believe that I might never see him again, I found a note on my table. It said:

To,
Professor Arronax
Aboard the Nautilus
November 16, 1867

Captain Nemo invites Professor Arronax for a hunting trip tomorrow in his own forests on Crespo Island. He looks forward with pleasure to the professor's companions joining in.

Captain Nemo,
Commander of the Nautilus

So, the next morning, I found myself walking into the dining room. Captain Nemo was there, waiting for me. "Professor," said he, "please feel free to share my breakfast. Eat well—you are not likely to eat dinner until very late."

"Captain," I said, "how is it that you own a forest when you have completely severed all your ties with society?"

"The forests of Crespo Island are no ordinary forests—they are underwater!" he replied. "And we will go there without getting our feet wet with our rifles in hand!"

"How so?" I asked, thoroughly confused.

"Man can walk underwater with ease," said Captain Nemo, "provided he has an oxygen supply. Usually, this is done by wearing an impervious suit and a metal helmet, which is attached to a tube that leads to the shore."

"A diving suit," I said.

"Correct!" confirmed the captain. "But instead of being fettered by a tube leading to the

Nautilus, we carry oxygen tanks on our backs. They contain oxygen to last us a good nine or ten hours."

"And how will the guns work?" I asked. "Are they going to be airguns?"

"Of course!" boomed Captain Nemo. "I cannot manufacture gunpowder. I use airguns with bullets that are charged with electricity, sending a shock through the fish which kills them instantly."

My mind was spinning with these revelations. When would Captain Nemo and his ingenuity fail to surprise me? Finishing my breakfast, I called my two companions. Together, we walked towards a cell near the machinery room to wear our suits.

A dozen diving suits hung from the partition. Seeing the suits hanging upon the wall, Ned Land turned up his nose with distaste. "You may do as you please, sir," he told me, "but I would never wear such a suit unless I was forced."

"Nobody will force you, Mr Ned," said Captain Nemo. "You may stay behind. Conseil, are you having second thoughts as well?"

"I will go wherever master goes," replied my faithful manservant.

Two crew members helped us into the heavy suits, which were made of India-rubber and copper. The suit consisted of trousers and a waistcoat. On our feet, we wore thick boots with leaden soles. One of the men handed me a gun with a large steel butt, which contained the compressed air required to push the bullets out.

Captain Nemo thrust his head into his helmet, and Conseil and I followed suit. It had three holes, which permitted us to see in every direction simply by turning our heads. I could breathe with ease using the tank on my back. It also had a lamp at the waist to light up the path ahead of us in the dark ocean.

It was impossible to even take a step in the heavy boots, but there was already a solution

for that. The crew members pushed the three of us into a little room. They screwed shut the watertight door behind us, leaving us in pitch darkness.

Water began pouring into the room with a loud hissing sound. A second door opened, leading us out into the open sea.

Chapter Nine

Crespo Island

Words are not enough to explain how it felt to walk on the ocean bed! I no longer felt the weight of my suit or boots, of the oxygen tank, or of my bulky helmet. The light at my waist was surprisingly powerful. I could clearly see objects even 150 yards away. Would you believe me when I say that, thirty feet under the sea, I could see as though I were in broad daylight?

We walked for an hour and a half, enjoying the sights around us. The ground underneath us had graduated into a thick, slimy mud. Suddenly, Captain Nemo stopped and waited

for us. He pointed to a dark, shadowy mass at a short distance.

"Crespo Island!" I thought; and I was right. We entered the forest that Captain Nemo had established as his own. It consisted of large tree-like plants, and I immediately noticed the unique position of their branches — not one was broken or bent. They all stretched up straight towards the surface of the ocean.

After four hours of walking, the captain signalled for us to stop. As all divers do, I felt an overwhelming desire for sleep. All of us fell asleep nearly instantly. I am not sure how long I slept, but when I awoke, Captain Nemo was already on his feet, looking at something a few steps away from me.

It was a monstrous sea-spider, more than three feet wide, ready to spring upon me! I could not help but shudder. A blow from the butt of the airgun was enough to knock it over. I saw the claws of the ugly crab-like creature convulse

in the air. After this incident, I was reminded to be on my guard — the ocean contains powerful creatures that could easily tear through my suit.

We walked through the forest until we reached a steep slope. At this point, Captain Nemo turned around — it was, presumably, the end of the forests of Crespo Island.

As we walked back to the *Nautilus*, we took a different route — a steeper and more difficult one. However, there were many shoals of fish along this path. Without warning, I saw the captain shoulder his gun, take aim and fire at something.

A creature fell to the ground at a distance. It was a beautiful sea otter, with chestnut-brown and silver fur. Captain Nemo threw the beast over his shoulder as we walked on. As we were walking through a shallow part, I had the privilege to witness one of the finest gunshots in the history of hunting.

A large bird with a considerable wingspan flew over the water above us. Captain Nemo raised his gun once more and fired at it. The creature fell straight into his hands — it was a fine albatross.

We continued walking, and by the time I spotted the faint glimmer of the *Nautilus*'s electric light, I felt like I could walk no longer. My oxygen tank was running out of oxygen, and I was eager to be back on the vessel. However, an accidental meeting would prolong my arrival for a while.

I was trailing behind the captain when he hurried towards me, pushing Conseil and me to the ground. He crouched down beside me, not moving a muscle. I raised my head over the bushes of algae to see what the matter was. Two great sharks were swimming by! Their skin cast phosphorescent gleams, making them appear as two huge shining masses. My blood froze — they were blue sharks, terrifying man-eaters with dull, glassy eyes and phosphorescent matter oozing from holes in their snouts.

I do not know whether Conseil had stopped to classify them under his helmet, but I can speak for myself when I say that I noticed their silver bellies and knife-like teeth not from the point-of-view of a naturalist, but a possible victim!

Thankfully, the fearsome creatures did not have a good sense of sight. They passed by without noticing us, so close that their fins brushed against us! We escaped unscathed from a danger that was far worse than meeting a tiger face-to-face in a jungle. It was a miracle!

Half an hour later, when we reached the *Nautilus*, I was so exhausted that as soon as the crew removed my diving suit, I retired to my room and immediately fell asleep.

The next morning, November 18, I had recovered from my exhaustion. I walked up to the platform only to see the second-in-command uttering his famous phrase. It probably meant something like "No land in sight."

Later, Captain Nemo made an appearance. Seemingly unaware of my presence, he began a series of astronomical observations. Once he had finished, he leaned his elbows on the railing and gazed absently at the ocean.

In the meanwhile, a number of strong, healthy crewmen appeared. They had come to draw up the fishing nets that had been laid the previous night. The men all seemed to be of different nationalities, but I could identify European traits in all of them. I saw Irishmen, Frenchmen, Slavs and a man who was a native of either Greece or Crete. They did not speak much, and when they did, they used the odd language which only the crew of the *Nautilus* seemed to know.

I reckon that they hauled in more than half a ton of fish, which comes as no surprise. The nets, having been laid down for several hours, are able to capture entire worlds of fish in between their strong threads. The vessel's electric light ensured that it could always attract more fish towards it when required. Thus, the *Nautilus* was never short of food.

The *Nautilus* continued on its course, moving in the south-east direction. On November 26, we crossed the tropic of Cancer. Every day, the windows would slide open, giving us a splendid view of the wonders outside. There was never a dull day, even though I did see very little of Captain Nemo.

On December 11, I was busy reading when Conseil appeared before me, saying, "I want master to look at something." So I followed him to the window and looked outside. I could see a huge, dark mass stranded in the ocean.

"It's a ship!" I gasped.

"Yes," confirmed Ned Land. "A sinking ship."

I could see the shattered planks of the ship floating in the sea. There were even some people clinging on for dear life — poor things! It was too late to help them.

We were stricken with sadness, our hearts beating fast. As we looked, we saw several hungry sharks rushing towards them. As the *Nautilus* passed by it, I read the following name on the ship's stern:

THE FLORIDA
SUNDERLAND, ENGLAND

Chapter Ten

Savages!

Witnessing that terrible sight was perhaps a sign of the misfortunes that the *Nautilus* would soon come to encounter. We were passing through the newly-formed islands in the southern hemisphere.

"In a few million years," I said to Captain Nemo, "these islands will combine into a single large continent."

"What the world needs is not a new continent," he replied coldly. "It needs new men!"

We then had to pass through the dicey Torres straits, which were spiked with countless

islands, islets, rocks and coral reefs, making the route nearly impossible to navigate.

But the *Nautilus* slid through the straits like magic. But then, we passed through a particularly thick knot of islands and islets. At three in the afternoon, during low tide, I felt a sudden shock pass through the vessel. The *Nautilus* had wedged itself on top of a reef.

Captain Nemo and his lieutenant were up on the platform, assessing the situation in their alien dialect. The vessel was completely undamaged. But, she could neither glide nor move off the rocks.

The captain approached me with a grim face. "An accident?" I asked.

"No," he replied. "Just an incident."

"An incident that might force you to live on land again! The *Nautilus* is quite stranded here, and the tides in the Pacific Ocean are not strong enough to make a difference."

The captain looked at me with a curious expression and said, "Even in these seas, the difference between high and low tide can rise to a yard and a half. In another two nights, it will be a full moon night. I'm sure the moon will bring in a strong enough tide then."

Ned was excited to hear this news. "There is an island nearby," he said. "On islands, there are trees; where there are trees, there are animals — which we can roast, mince and feast upon."

"I agree with Ned," said Conseil. "Could not master ask for permission to go hunting?"

When I asked the captain, to my greatest surprise, he relented. He did not even ask me to promise that we would return to the vessel! However, we were not in Europe. Escaping in New Guinea would be too dangerous. It was better to be a prisoner of Captain Nemo than to fall into the hands of hostile natives.

That evening, armed with guns and hatchets, the three of us boarded the *Nautilus'* longboat.

Ned Land could hardly contain his joy. "Meat! We are going to eat meat!" he said gleefully.

In half an hour, we had reached the sandy shores of the island. It was so good to put my feet on solid ground! There were huge trees with trunks over 200 feet high. There were plants of every kind, forming a huge green canopy.

Ned Land immediately found a coconut tree, beat down some of its fruit, broke them open, lapped up the milk and ate the flesh with great enthusiasm.

Venturing deeper into the island, we found a variety of vegetables. A particularly delightful find was breadfruit, which when cooked has the taste and texture of bread. After cooking ourselves a little feast, we made our way back to the *Nautilus* armed with vegetables of all kinds.

The next day, we returned to the island, this time hoping to catch some game. We explored a different part of the island that day, following the torrents of water. We found a few birds, but they refused to let us approach them. This made me realise that the birds were used to humans.

Surprisingly, it was Conseil who got us breakfast — he brought down a white pigeon and a wood-pigeon with a skilful double shot. We plucked these and roasted them over some dead wood. We enjoyed them with some breadfruit.

But Ned Land was still in the mood to catch something that walked on four feet! At 2 o'clock, his wish was fulfilled — he brought down a mighty hog. Later, Conseil and Ned managed to shoot a dozen small kangaroos!

"What if we do not return to the *Nautilus* this evening?" asked Conseil.

"What if we do not return at all?" replied Ned.

But before I could put in my two cents, a sharp stone fell at our feet.

"Stones do not usually fall from the sky," said Conseil.

Another carefully aimed stone sent the pigeon leg flying from Conseil's hand. The three of us rose to our feet, shouldering our guns.

"Apes, maybe?" cried Ned Land.

"Not quite," said Conseil. "They are savages."

"To the longboat!" I shouted, hurrying to the sea.

About twenty natives, armed with slingshots and bows, approached us from a copse to the right. They didn't run, but threw stones and arrows by the second.

Ned Land was not willing to leave behind his game. Despite carrying a boar and a dozen kangaroos, he ran fast. In two minutes, we were in the longboat, pushing it off into the sea.

We had hardly gone a few feet when about a hundred savages, howling and gesticulating with rage, entered the water up to their waists. We rowed with all our might, and in twenty minutes, we were on board the *Nautilus*. I immediately went over to Captain Nemo, who was playing the piano with great concentration. When I told him the news, he did not even raise an eyebrow.

"So it surprises you that, having set foot on a strange island, you ran into savages?" he asked mockingly. "How many were there?"

"A hundred at least."

"Professor Arronax," said the captain. "Even if all the savages of Papua assemble on the shore, the *Nautilus* will have nothing to worry about."

He went back to his piano, soon forgetting that I was standing beside him. I dared not disturb him once again, so I went up to the platform to survey the situation. It was already dark outside. I could see that the savages were all on the beach, their fires lit up.

The next morning, I went to the platform to see that the savages had brought out their canoes. In less than half an hour, they would be at the *Nautilus*! I rushed to Captain Nemo.

He was performing some extremely complex algebraic calculations.

"I am sorry to disturb you," I said, "but the savages are surrounding us. In a few minutes, they will be able to climb up onto the hull."

"Then we must close the hatches," said the captain, as calm as ever. He pressed an electric button that sent the order to the ship's crew.

"It is done," said Captain Nemo. "The hatches are closed. The savages can do no harm to us—not when the bullets of the *Abraham Lincoln* failed!"

"But Captain, we are still in danger," I said. "We will have to open the hatches to renew the air soon. The savages can easily enter then."

"Then let them," said the captain. "I see no reason why even a single one of them should lose their lives for our sakes."

Soon enough, the savages arrived, trampling upon the platform and chanting loudly. They

remained there all day but Captain Nemo chose to ignore them. Tonight was to be the full moon night, when we would escape. I hoped that the savages would not dampen our plans.

When the night arrived, I was filled with anxiety as I watched the hatches open. As soon as they did, twenty horrible faces appeared. But when they touched the railing, they were struck by an invisible force, sending them running away and screaming.

I put the puzzle pieces together — the rail had been charged with electricity. Touching it could have been fatal, had Captain Nemo discharged a higher voltage of current.

Some of us had a hearty laugh at the savages' expense. Then, the *Nautilus* was lifted on a wave, dislodged from her rocky bed and swept into the sea.

Chapter Eleven

The Coral Graveyard

To make up for lost time, the *Nautilus* seemed to travel faster than ever. We were making our way towards the Indian Ocean. Things were going smoothly until a strange incident brought us back to the grim reality of our situation.

On the morning of January 18, I went up to the platform just as the second-in-command was scanning the horizon. But instead of his usual utterance, the man used a different phrase — something equally incomprehensible.

Almost immediately, Captain Nemo appeared on the platform, looking towards the horizon keenly. When he lowered his telescope, he

looked as though he was possessed by a very strong emotion.

A heated discussion ensued. When the captain finally looked towards me, I felt as though I did not recognise him. "Professor Arronax," he said. "The time has come for you to honour your promise. You must be locked up with your companions until I release you."

"As you wish," I replied, "but may I ask you one question?"

"No."

When I broke the news to my friends, Ned Land's reaction was that of outrage. But there was no time for arguments. Four members of the crew escorted us to the same cell in which we had spent our first night on the *Nautilus*. There was breakfast on the table, and we ate in silence. Just then, the light in the cell went out, leaving us in total darkness.

Ned Land soon fell asleep. It struck me as rather odd when Conseil immediately followed suit. "We've been drugged …!" I gasped. My brain was becoming stupefied and my eyelids heavy. Before I knew it, I was asleep, too.

When I woke up, I was surprised to find myself in my own room. I checked whether my door was locked. The door opened easily.

I found Ned and Conseil awaiting me on the platform. They were as clueless as me. The day went on as usual. At 2 o'clock in the afternoon, Captain Nemo came to my room. His face was etched with fatigue.

"Are you a doctor, professor?" he asked.

I was so surprised by the question that I almost didn't answer. "Why … why, yes!" I finally replied. "I am a doctor and a surgeon. I practised for several years before I decided to join the museum."

"Very well, professor," he said. "Will you consent to treat one of my men?"

"Of course," I replied. "Lead the way."

Captain Nemo guided me into a cabin near the crew's quarters. There, on a bed, lay a man of about my age. He was not just ill, he was severely wounded. His head was covered in bloody bandages. I undid them carefully.

It was a horrible wound. His skull was shattered by some deadly weapon, leaving his brain exposed. The brain itself was injured badly. I felt his pulse — it beat irregularly. I dressed his wounds, readjusted his bandage and returned to Captain Nemo.

"What caused this wound?" I asked.

"Never mind that," said the captain, evading my question. "What's the verdict? You may speak freely — he does not understand French."

I sighed. "He will die within two hours. I can do nothing to save him."

Upon hearing this, Captain Nemo lowered his head, his eyes glistening with tears. I left, taking one last look at the poor dying man.

The next morning, Captain Nemo invited us to join him on yet another excursion.

I accepted his invitation, as did Conseil and, surprisingly, Ned Land. We — along with

Captain Nemo and a dozen crew members — were helped into our diving suits and released into the sea.

We walked into a beautiful coral kingdom. There were thousands of varieties in countless vivid colours. I was tempted to touch them, but if I so much as brushed against these living flowers, the whole colony would retract into their cases, transforming the colourful colony into a block of stony knobs.

After two hours of walking, Captain Nemo halted. His crew formed a semicircle around him. Six of them carried an oblong-shaped object on their shoulders.

On observing the ground around me, I saw that it was raised at intervals by limestone-like deposits. A coral cross stood on a pedestal of piled-up rocks. On Captain Nemo's signal, one of the men came forward and began digging a hole with a pickaxe that he took from his belt.

This glade was a graveyard, and the crewman was digging a grave for the man who had died the day before.

When the man was buried, Captain Nemo and his men knelt at the grave, extending their hands as a last farewell. Then, we returned to the *Nautilus*.

"So, the man rests near his companions, in the coral graveyard?" I asked Captain Nemo.

"Yes," he replied. "Forgotten by everyone, but not us." Burying his face in his hands, he tried to suppress a sob.

"Your dead sleep quietly and peacefully, Captain," I said. "Out of the reach of sharks."

"Yes, sir," replied the captain, gravely. "Of sharks and men!"

Chapter Twelve

Pearl Diving

Two more months passed by as the *Nautilus* entered the waters of the Indian Ocean. On February 28, 1868, Captain Nemo came to me with a unique proposition.

"The island of Ceylon is noted for its pearl fisheries. Would you like to visit one of them?"

I agreed immediately, and told my friends about this good piece of news.

They were delighted. The next morning, at 4 o'clock, I met Captain Nemo. "Shall we go?" he asked.

"What about our diving suits?" I inquired.

"We will wear them in the boat," he replied. "It will take us to the exact spot we need to get to, so that we will have less walking to do."

We met Conseil and Ned at the platform. Five crewmen were waiting in the boat. They rowed us to the spot and dropped an anchor into the ocean. We put on our diving suits and helmets, but there was no use for the lamps as the sun rays could easily penetrate the water. Instead of guns, we carried steel blades in our belts. Ned also carried his harpoon.

Then, we dropped into the ocean and followed Captain Nemo. He pointed to us heaps upon heaps of oysters in the oyster banks. Ned Land quickly filled up a net at his belt with the finest specimens he could find. The ground was gradually rising, and at points, if I raised my arm, it would be above the surface of the sea.

Then we entered into a cave-like structure, which immediately shrouded us in darkness. I could distinguish arches above me and huge natural pillars around. The captain pointed downwards to a gigantic oyster. It must have weighed at least 300 kilograms.

Captain Nemo then proceeded to stick his blade in between the two shells of the oyster, trying to force them open. There, between the folds of flesh, I saw a pearl the size of a coconut! I extended my hand to touch it, but the captain stopped me. He withdrew his blade, causing the oyster to clamp shut. Captain Nemo wanted to leave the pearl undisturbed, allowing it to grow bigger and bigger.

After ten minutes, Captain Nemo suddenly stopped in his tracks. He crouched behind a rock, beckoning for us to do the same.

About five yards away, a shadow appeared, sinking to the ground. The troubling thought of sharks flashed through my mind, but it was no sea animal — just a man.

He was a poor Indian fisherman, by the looks of it. He had come early in the season, so as

to beat competition. His canoe was anchored above him, which he was tied to with a rope. Reaching the bottom, he would fill his bag with oysters, swim up, empty the bag and restart the same operation.

Suddenly, I saw an expression of terror flash on the man's face. He made to swim desperately to the surface of the sea.

A gigantic shadow appeared just above him — a shark! Its jaws were wide open and its eyes were ablaze. One thrash of its tail struck the Indian in his chest and to the ground. The shark was about to pounce on him when I saw Captain Nemo rise, dagger in hand, and walk up to the monster, ready for a fight.

The shark, sensing its new enemy, turned away from the fisherman and made straight for the captain, who threw himself to one side, avoiding the collision. He buried his blade into the shark's side.

The shark roared. Blood gushed from its wound. It unhinged its jaws like a pair of industrial shears. The captain would have died if Ned Land had not sprung up and struck the shark with his harpoon. Struck in the heart, the shark struggled in its last moments, violently convulsing, and then was still.

Ned Land disentangled Captain Nemo, who straight away went to the Indian fisherman. Scooping him up in his arms, he swam to the surface with a sharp kick of his heel. The three of us followed suit, reaching the fisherman's boat in a few seconds.

Captain Nemo tried to revive the man. The man stirred and opened his eyes. What a great surprise he must have felt to see four great copper heads staring back at him! His surprise only increased when Captain Nemo reached into his pocket and placed a bag of pearls in his hand.

Back on board the longboat, we relieved ourselves of the heavy helmets. Captain Nemo's first words were to Ned Land.

"Thank you, Mr Land," he said.

"I owed you that," replied the Canadian.

The ghost of a smile appeared upon the captain's lips, but he did not reply.

On our way back to the *Nautilus*, we came across the carcass of the horrible blacktip reef shark. It was over twenty-five feet long. Its mouth—which took up more than a third of its body—was lined with six rows of sharp, triangular teeth. While we watched, a herd of sharks zoomed towards the carcass, fighting each other for the pieces.

When I looked back on the incident, I drew two things—one, that Captain Nemo was extremely courageous, and two, that his heart still swelled with love for humanity.

When I brought this up with him, he seemed moved. "That Indian," he said, "is a native of an oppressed land—just like me!"

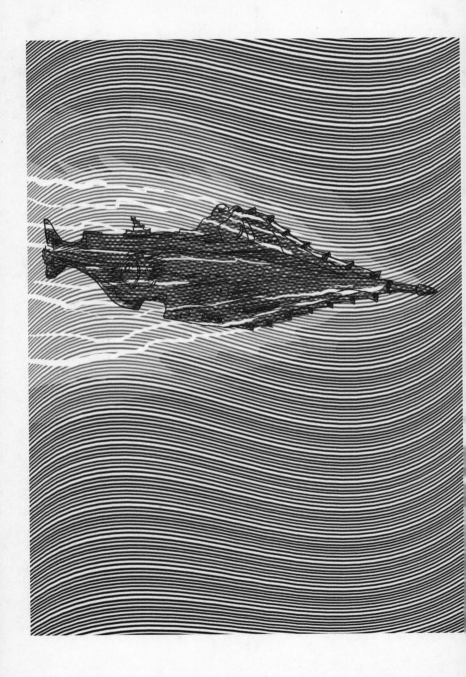

Chapter Thirteen

The Arabian Tunnel

Soon, the *Nautilus* made its way towards the seas of Africa. By this point, we had already covered 7,500 leagues from our starting point. Now, we seemed to be headed towards the Persian Gulf — which was strange! The Persian Gulf was a dead-end. As soon as I saw Captain Nemo, I asked him about this.

"Don't worry," said the captain, "in two days, we shall be in the Mediterranean Sea."

"That's impossible!" I cried. "The *Nautilus* would have to go dangerously fast if we have to go around all of Africa in two days!"

"Who told you that we are going around Africa?" said the captain.

"Well, unless the *Nautilus* can sail on dry land and pass over the continent —"

"Or under it, Professor Arronax!"

"I am not sure I understand you," I said.

"A long time ago, Professor," said the captain, "Mother Nature created a passage under the continent what today, men are trying to make above it."

"Oh! A tunnel?"

"Yes," said Captain Nemo, "a tunnel which I have named the Arabian Tunnel. It takes us underneath the Suez and into the Gulf of Pelusium in the Mediterranean."

"Did you discover it by chance?" I asked.

"More by reasoning," he replied. "You see, I noticed that fish of the same kind were present in both the Red Sea and the Mediterranean. So I passed copper rings through the tails of a large number of fish in the Suez, and threw them back into the water. When I went to the Mediterranean, I caught these same ringed fish. So I began to look for the tunnel. Soon, you will have the chance to pass through it, too!"

A day after this conversation, I found myself on the platform with Ned and Conseil. Suddenly, Ned sat up straight.

"Do you see that?" he asked.

"Yes, I did!" replied Conseil. "It looks just like a mermaid!"

"No, not a mermaid, lad," I said. "It's actually a dugong."

"Order *Sirenia*, group *Pisciforma*, subclass *Monodelphia*, class *Mammalia*, branch *Vertebrata*," Conseil replied.

If Ned Land had had his harpoon at hand, he would have already thrown it at the creature. At that very moment, Captain Nemo came up. Following Ned Land's line of vision, he saw the dugong.

"You can harpoon it," he said. "But take great care not to miss. Dugongs are known to have a fierce temper."

Soon, seven crewmen came up, one holding a harpoon. They let down the longboat into the sea. Captain Nemo did not join us.

We rowed rapidly towards the dugong until we were only a few cable lengths away from it. Ned, holding his harpoon, stood at the front.

The dugong was of more than seven yards long. It seemed to be sleeping upon the waves, making it easier to capture.

When we were within six yards of the animal, Ned Land threw his harpoon. Suddenly, we heard a hissing sound, and the dugong disappeared. Surprisingly, Ned Land seemed to have missed his target!

"Curse it!" swore the Canadian.

We retrieved his weapon and went in search of the animal once more. When it came to the surface for air, it moved with great speed.

Whenever we got close enough to harpoon, it would dive again, making it impossible for us to strike.

We pursued it for an hour, but with no success. Just when I began to think it impossible to capture, the animal resurfaced and threw itself upon us, possessed with the idea of revenge.

The boat received a violent shove, but thankfully, it did not get overturned. Ned Land threw his harpoon at it, and this time, it struck the heart. Had he not been successful, I shudder to think how our hunt would have ended. It required very strong pulleys to hoist the dugong onto the platform. It weighed 500 kilograms!

The following night, we entered into the Arabian Tunnel. In a matter of less than a few minutes, we had reached the Mediterranean.

Chapter Fourteen

The Greek Islands

The next morning, once Ned Land was convinced that he was indeed in the Mediterranean Sea, he began once again to talk of escape.

I confess that I was in a dilemma. I did not want to restrict my friends' freedom. And yet, I had no desire to leave the *Nautilus*. "Are you bored, Ned?" I asked. "Answer me honestly."

Ned crossed his arms. "Honestly," he said, "I am not bored. I am not sorry to have come here. But what begins also has to end."

A heated discussion followed. We just could not see eye-to-eye! Finally, we agreed that it would be best to escape while we were near the

coast of Europe. When this opportunity would come, I did not know.

As the days went by, I noticed that we were sailing towards the ancient island of Crete. At the time when I had boarded the *Abraham Lincoln*, the whole island was rebelling against its tyrannical rulers, the Ottoman Turks. But being at sea, I had no idea what had happened of the revolution, and I doubt Captain Nemo knew of it, either.

As I was looking through the glass panes one day, I spotted a diver among the waves. I realised it was not a corpse, but a living man, swimming vigorously.

I turned to Captain Nemo, alarmed. "A man!" I cried. "We must rescue him!"

The captain leaned against the window. To my great surprise, he signalled at the diver, who signalled back. Then, the man swam back to the surface of the sea and did not return.

"Don't worry," said the captain. "That's Nicolas, fondly known as *Il Pesce*. He is a diver of the first order."

Then, Captain Nemo did something curious. He went to a cabinet in a corner which bore the *Nautilus'* monogram. He opened the cabinet, which contained a large number of gold ingots!

Captain Nemo took out the ingots and arranged them inside a chest. I estimated that it held about 1,000 kilograms of gold. He closed the chest and wrote an address on the lid. The characters seemed to be Modern Greek.

Then, his crew of four men appeared promptly, and pushed the chest out with great difficulty. I heard them hoist it up to the platform outside.

Captain Nemo turned to me. "You were saying, Professor Arronax?" he asked.

"I wasn't saying anything," I replied.

"Then, sir, with your permission, I will bid you goodnight."

I went to my cabin feeling most confused. What did the diver have to do with the gold ingots? Later in the night, I felt us rise to the ocean's surface. I heard the sound of footsteps on the platform — the longboat was being launched.

Two hours later, I heard noises of the same comings and goings. The longboat was reattached into its socket and the vessel plunged back under the surface. Without a doubt, the crewmen had transported Captain Nemo's gold to an address on land. But to whom?

When I related these events to Conseil and Ned the next day, they were as taken aback as I was. At about 5 o'clock in the afternoon, as I was working in the library, I began to feel extremely hot. I wondered if there had been a fire onboard.

I was about to get up and investigate when Captain Nemo entered the room. "42° centigrade," he said.

"I've noticed," I replied. "I don't think I'd be able to stand it if it got any hotter."

"It won't get hotter," replied the captain. "If it did, we could always retreat away from the source of heat."

"And what is this source of heat?"

"The underwater volcanoes, of course," said Captain Nemo. "We're sailing through boiling water!"

I looked outside the panels. The sea was completely white. Steaming fumes wove around the bubbling waves. I placed my hand against one of the windows, but it was so hot that I had to snatch it back.

"The seas near the Greek island of Santorini are known to have active volcanoes," said Captain Nemo.

The *Nautilus* had stopped moving. The heat had risen to unbearable levels, and the sea was turning red instead of white. I could smell the sulphur even through the thick walls of the vessel.

"We can't stay in this boiling water any longer," I said.

"No, we cannot," replied Nemo. He gave an order, and the vessel backed away from the heat. Fifteen minutes later, we were breathing fresh air at the surface.

Then, I was struck by a sinister thought. If Ned had chosen to escape in these waters, we would have surely been cooked. The next day, the *Nautilus* made its way ahead, leaving the Greek islands behind.

Chapter Fifteen

Escape

We passed through the Mediterranean at such speed, that any attempts at escape were futile. Not surprisingly, this put Ned in a foul mood. Before long, we had already entered the Atlantic Ocean. We had done 10,000 leagues in a span of three and a half months.

One day, I found Ned Land in my cabin, looking rather sullen. We had not been able to escape when we were at the Mediterranean, and he was visibly disappointed.

"Don't blame yourself, Ned," I said. "We will soon find a way to escape."

But Ned Land had a plan of his own. "We'll do it this evening," he said. "We'll be only a few miles off the coast of Spain. It will be cloudy. The wind is blowing towards the shore. We have near-perfect conditions."

I could not say anything against his reasonable arguments.

"We'll do it this evening," he repeated, "at 9 o'clock. Conseil and I will go to the central shaft. You will stay in the library and wait for my signal. There are provisions in the longboat. So everything is set."

"The sea is rough," I said quietly.

"It's a small risk," replied Ned. "If everything goes our way, tonight at ten or eleven, we will be on solid ground. I'll see you this evening."

With those words, the Canadian left, leaving me dumbstruck. I could do nothing but carry out the plan and hope for the best.

I stayed in my cabin all day long, hoping to avoid Captain Nemo. I was torn between my

desire for freedom and my regret at leaving this marvellous vessel.

At dinner, I ate very little. As I passed Captain Nemo's cabin later, I noticed with astonishment that his door was ajar. I instinctively stepped back. I didn't want to run into him. However, I could not hear any sounds from inside. Curiosity got the better of me, and I pushed the door open.

Some hangings on the wall caught my eye — things I hadn't noticed on my first visit. There were portraits of great men from history — George Washington, Abraham Lincoln, Thaddeus Kosciusko of Poland, Daniel O'Connell of Ireland and several others.

Why did Captain Nemo identify so strongly with these heroes? Was he a freedom-fighter of some kind?

Just that minute, the clock struck eight, snapping me out of my musings. I shuddered violently and hurried outside his cabin.

A few minutes before 9 o'clock, I proceeded to the library, where I waited for Ned's signal. Just then, the door opened, and Captain Nemo appeared before us.

"Ah, Professor Arronax," he said in a friendly tone. "I've been looking for you! Do you know your Spanish history?"

I was so stunned by his appearance, as well as his odd question, that I was speechless. After grappling with my tongue for a few moments, I managed to utter a reply.

"Not too well, Captain."

"Ah!" he said. "Then you're in for a fine lesson today."

The captain sat me down next to him. I tried to sink into the shadows so that he would not notice how scared I looked. But he seemed to be lost in his own thoughts.

"You see," he began, "In the sixteenth century, many countries were trying to attack the country of Spain—England, Holland,

Austria and even your own France."

I could only nod silently to what he said.

"It was difficult for Spain to withstand these enemies as they did not have much of an army," he continued. "But one thing it did have was lots and lots of money. But this money would only reach the country if the trading ships came back from America."

"Ah," I said. "And for that, they would have to risk being attacked by the enemies."

"Correct," said Captain Nemo. "The fleet of Spanish ships was supposed to dock at a port called Cadiz, but they learnt that some English ships had already attacked it. So, they made a hasty decision to port at the Bay of Vigo ... are you following me?"

"Completely," I chimed in, still unsure as to why I was being given this history lesson.

"Now, the ships could have unloaded their treasures at the Bay of Vigo easily before the English ships could catch up with them. But

the authorities at Cadiz did not like this, as they would lose money from this arrangement.

Because of this, the Spanish fleet was attacked by the English. The Spaniards fought courageously, but in the end, they were no match for the English. But instead of allowing the wealth to go into enemy hands, the Spanish admiral burned all the ships. They sank to the bottom of the ocean — safe from the English."

Captain Nemo beckoned me toward the windows. All around the *Nautilus*, I could see crewmen dressed in diving suits, clearing away half-rotted trunks and barrels from the ancient shipwrecks. These trunks contained all kinds of treasure.

I understood. We were deep under the Bay of Vigo, where the Spanish treasure lay. And since nobody else in the world could reach this deep, Captain Nemo was able to claim it all.

"I cannot help but feel a little sorry for the thousands of people who could have benefitted

from a fair distribution of this wealth," I said. I could see that Captain Nemo was wounded.

"Sir," he said. "What makes you think that the wealth does not go to those who need it? Do you think I take this treasure out of selfishness? Do you think I'm not aware that there are people suffering? Don't you understand?"

Captain Nemo suddenly stopped short. But I had understood already. The stern captain still had a heart that throbbed for human suffering. That is why he had delivered those ingots to the diver near Crete, where the people were at war!

Chapter Sixteen

The Lost Continent

The next morning, Ned Land entered my cabin with an expression of great disappointment. "That damned captain had to come to a halt just as we were going to escape," he said.

"Yes, he had business with his bank vault," I said, and explained the events of the previous night. I hoped that it would put the Canadian off from trying to escape. But it had no such effect.

"It's not over yet," he said. "My first harpoon missed, but we'll succeed the next time. As soon as this evening, if it is possible."

But the compass told us that we were heading towards the south-west—away from

Europe. Soon, we could see nothing but the immense blue sea. Ned Land had no choice but to abandon his plans.

At 11 o'clock that evening, Captain Nemo visited my cabin. "Would you be interested in a night-time excursion?" he asked. "I warn you, this will be a long, difficult walk."

"That only increases my interest," I said. "I will surely come."

As we slipped into our diving suits, I saw that nobody except the captain and me were to go on this excursion. The oxygen tanks were strapped onto our backs, but not the lamps.

I commented on this to Captain Nemo. "They will be useless to us," he replied.

Before I could argue, the captain had already screwed on his metal helmet. I followed suit, and soon, we were at the floor of the Atlantic.

The waters were extremely dark, but Captain Nemo pointed to a reddish, shimmering spot in the distance, about two miles away. It lit up our path with an eerie glow, and I could see why our lamps would have been useless.

We walked together towards the flame. As we walked, the seafloor rose higher and higher. As we walked, I heard a pitter-patter above my head. It was a heavy rainfall thundering upon the ocean! I instinctively worried that I would get soaked. I could not help smiling at this thought.

After walking for an hour, the ground turned rocky. The stones were in a symmetry that told me that humans had something to do with it.

Meanwhile, the reddish glow had expanded and inflamed the whole horizon. Was it an underwater furnace? Our path grew brighter. The red glow had turned white and I could now see that it was coming from a tall peak.

We began to climb up the mountain, but I did not feel exhausted. We leapt across abysses and walked on wobbling tree trunks that acted as bridges. Despite my heavy clothing, I climbed the steepest slopes with all the nimbleness of a mountain goat!

Two hours after we had started, we were only 100 feet away from the peak. My blood curdled as I watched a pair of enormous antenna cross my path, or saw a gruesome pincer snap shut in the shadows. A thousand specks of light glittered in the darkness — they were the eyes of the gigantic creatures crawling all around us in the caves and crevices.

Then, we arrived at a flat piece of land where there were huge stones piled upon each other in the form of what looked like palaces and temples. Covering them were shrouds of plants — not ivy, but algae and fucus.

I followed Captain Nemo to the peak, which was only around ten metres wide. I looked down from the peak. The slope we had climbed up from was not high, but on the other side, it was twice as high. The mountain was a volcano. Fifty feet below its peak, a wide

crater gushed out streams of lava that lit up the area brilliantly.

Beneath me, I could see a ruined ancient city. I detected traces of Tuscan architecture — here, the vague form of a Parthenon; there, the remnants of a wharf.

Captain Nemo tapped my shoulder. Then, picking up a chalky stone, he wrote the following word on the black rock:

ATLANTIS

Atlantis, the ancient continent mentioned in historical texts; the continent whose existence had been denied by philosophers and scientists; the continent that was believed to have sunk many thousand years ago!

We stayed there for an hour, taking in the sights. A few rays of moonlight pierced through the water, lighting up the lost continent. Even though it lasted only a few moments, the effect was indescribable. When Captain Nemo beckoned me to follow him back down, I did so with a very heavy heart.

Chapter Seventeen

More Excursions

One day, I climbed onto the platform, but found myself in total darkness. Was it night time? No! Not even the night was as pitch black.

I heard Nemo's voice from the darkness. "Is that you, Professor Arronax?"

"Captain Nemo," I replied. "Where are we?"

"Underground, Professor."

"And the *Nautilus* is still afloat?" I asked.

"Yes. Wait for the light to come on, and maybe you'll find some answers," he said.

When the electric light came on, I saw that the *Nautilus* was floating by a wharf-like formation.

"We are in the heart of an extinct volcano," said Captain Nemo. "The sea passes through its base, and we enter through the same opening."

"But why?" I asked. "The *Nautilus* does not need a resting place."

"But it does need coal!" exclaimed the captain. "I get it from this volcano."

"Ah," I replied. "So, will I get to see your crewmen at work?"

"Not this time," said Captain Nemo. "I want to replenish my stocks in one working day. Then we'll resume our voyage. So, you can spend the day exploring the volcano."

So Ned, Conseil and I set out to explore. There was a sandy beach in between the water entering the volcano and its tall walls. We walked along this shore, our footsteps sending the sand flying into the air.

We climbed upwards, towards the mouth of the volcano. As we walked, the path became steeper and narrower. There were jagged rocks

strewed along the path, making it even more difficult. At some parts, we had to even crawl on our bellies.

When we reached a height of about 250 feet, we could go no further. At this point, we could see all kinds of shrubs and even a few trees emerging from the cracks in the walls.

"Look, a beehive!" said Ned, pointing at it. "There are bees buzzing around it, too!"

Naturally, Ned Land wanted to draw out the honey and make a meal of it. He mixed sulphur with some dry leaves, set them on fire and used the smoke to drive the bees away.

Once the buzzing had died down completely, he broke apart the hive.

It was a large hive, and it yielded a large quantity of sweet honey. Ned Land filled up his haversack with the honeycombs. "When I soak this honey with the paste of breadfruit," he said, "I will serve you a delicious piece of cake."

We continued our stroll, and soon enough, I saw that the bees were not the only non-human animals in the volcano. There were birds of prey near the top.

Ned Land, for lack of bullets, began to throw stones at them. After several attempts, he managed to wound a large bustard. We reached the *Nautilus* just as the crewmen had finished loading it up with sodium. The *Nautilus* was ready to depart.

However, Captain Nemo gave no orders to that effect. I believed that he was waiting for nightfall, so that his passageway would truly remain a secret.

When I woke up the next day, we were back in the Atlantic Ocean, sailing a few metres beneath its surface. Our voyage continued, and by March 13, we had covered 13,000 leagues.

We were sailing above some of the deepest parts of the ocean known to humankind, and Captain Nemo was eager to take the *Nautilus* to these depths for his studies. To do this, the

Nautilus had to exert its full power. Its hull quivered as it sank lower and lower.

Soon, even the small tubeworms and seashells vanished from sight. We reached a depth of 16,000 meters — where no man had ever gone before!

"How sad it is that we can only preserve these sights in our memories!" I sighed, looking at the otherworldly sight.

"We could easily take a photograph!" said Captain Nemo.

Before I could bat an eyelid, a crewman walked in, carrying a camera. In a few seconds, we had a negative of the scene.

"Let's go back up," said the captain. "Hold on tight!"

Before I knew it, I was hurled towards the carpet. The *Nautilus* rose with lightning speed, shooting up like a balloon in air. In four minutes, we were back at the surface of the ocean, sending the waves thrashing around us violently.

Chapter Eighteen

To The South Pole

The *Nautilus* kept moving southwards, and I could not help but wonder about our next destination. Were we going to the South Pole? That would be foolishness.

One day, we were seated at the platform when the Canadian spotted a large baleen whale. "Look! It's coming towards us!" he said, his voice tinged with excitement. "I'm going to ask for permission to hunt it."

He leaped down the hatch to look for Captain Nemo. Moments later, the two of them reappeared on the platform. Captain Nemo observed the herd of whales. "They're southern

whales," he said. "We have no use for whale oil on this ship. I will not allow killing for the sake of killing."

Ned Land gritted his teeth and walked away.

"The southern whales have enough enemies as it is," continued Captain Nemo. "Can you see those blackish specks moving about there?"

"Yes, Captain," I answered.

"Those are sperm whales. They're cruel, destructive beasts and we should exterminate them to save the lives of the southern whales."

"Well, we still have time ..."

"Let's not run any risks," said the Captain, cutting me off. "The *Nautilus* is equipped with a steel spur that's just as deadly as Mr Land's harpoon, I believe."

Ned Land did not even bother giving us the slightest reaction. Attacking whales with a spur! Whoever heard of such nonsense?

There was just enough time for the *Nautilus* to act. I felt the beats of our propeller getting faster

as we went ahead. By the time we reached, the battle between the whales had already begun.

What a struggle! The *Nautilus* was a fearsome harpoon in the hands of Captain Nemo.

After a long battle, the sea grew tranquil again. We rose to the surface and rushed onto the platform. There were floating carcasses all around us. Among the sperm whales also lay a southern whale. We had been too late to save the poor animal, which was still holding her calf at her fin.

The *Nautilus* approached the corpse, and two crewmen climbed onto the whale, filling their casks with her milk.

Captain Nemo offered me a cup of the milk. It was still warm, and as delicious as cow's milk.

We continued to be south-bound, and on March 14, I spotted a floating ice sheet. Ned was already used to the sight of icebergs, but Conseil and I were awestruck.

Soon, all we could see was ice all around. I could not see how we would overcome this obstacle. By this point, everything seemed to be frozen—even sound!

"If Captain Nemo goes any farther, he'll be a superman," said Ned.

"How so?" I asked.

"Nobody can navigate through this. Nemo may be powerful, but damn it, he isn't more powerful than nature."

"I have to admit, I am curious to see what is behind these mountains of ice."

"More ice!" said Ned sourly.

Indeed, the *Nautilus* seemed well and truly stuck. Usually, when one cannot go further, one has the option of returning in one's tracks. But here, it was impossible to do so, because the thick ice formed within minutes, blocking our pathways. If the *Nautilus* continued to be stationary, it would soon be covered in ice itself!

One day, I chanced upon the captain upon the platform and voiced my doubts to him.

"Oh Professor!" said Nemo. "You never change! Not only will the *Nautilus* float, it will go much farther south than this!"

"To the pole?" I asked.

"Yes, sir, to the pole!" said the captain. "The Antarctic pole."

"Have you ever been there before?"

"No, sir," he admitted. "We are going to discover it together."

"Sure, Captain," I said, my tone laced with sarcasm. "Let us forge ahead! Let us shatter this ice bank! Let us blow over it!"

"No, not over it," said the captain, "but underneath it!"

Now it was my turn to be surprised. The *Nautilus* was to go underneath the ice. For even though the ocean's surface was frozen solid, water still flowed underneath.

195

The *Nautilus'* pumps forced air down into the tanks and stored it under great pressure. Some men climbed onto the vessel's sides and cracked loose the ice holding it in place.

Soon, they re-entered vessel, the hatches were closed and the *Nautilus* dove underwater.

We zipped through the water easily enough, but when it was time to surface, we met with an obstacle. The ice near the pole was much thicker – there was about 4,000 feet of it between us and the surface of the ocean.

The *Nautilus* got to work. Using as much force as possible, it would bump its spur into the ice sheet, cracking it bit by bit. Finally, at 6 o'clock in the morning of March 19, Captain Nemo brought me the good news.

"Open sea!" he said.

I rushed up to the platform. Yes, it was open sea! "Are we at the pole?" I asked the captain.

"I don't know yet," he answered. "We'll find our position by noon."

To the south of the *Nautilus*, there rose one single islet amongst the floating ice sheets. Nemo, Conseil and I got into the longboat along with two crewmen, who rowed us to the shore.

"Sir," I told Captain Nemo, "You should have the honour of being the first one to step on this particular shore."

"With pleasure!" he said. "And for once I am happy to set foot on land, as nobody else has set a footstep here before."

With those words, he leaped lightly on the islet. Conseil and I followed suit, leaving the two crewmen in the longboat. We spotted a variety of seals and walruses on the shore. Not being used to humans, they did not cower away from us. I could hear the calls of petrel and albatross.

"It is fortunate that Ned Land did not accompany us," said Conseil. "He would have killed every animal in sight!"

We climbed up to the tallest spot we could find, hoping that the sun would show its face to us. Captain Nemo had carried a spyglass and his chronometer. My heart was pounding with anticipation. If the lower half of the sun's disk disappeared just as the chronometer said it was noon, we were at the South Pole.

"Noon!" I called, reading the chronometer.

"The South Pole!" answered Captain Nemo. He handed me the spyglass, and I saw it for myself—the horizon cut the sun into exactly two halves.

Captain Nemo unfurled a black flag with a golden 'N' emblazoned upon it. Thus, he had marked this South Pole for himself.

Having conquered the South Pole, our worries were not quite over. One night, while making our way out of the Antarctic, I was awoken by a violent collision which hurled me across the room. The *Nautilus* had not only run aground in a tunnel of ice, but it was stuck in a tilted position.

The crew was already working on straightening the vessel, and there was nothing to do but wait. Finally, we managed to sit upright and break free of the ice. The ceiling lights were out, yet we could see clearly because the ice reflected the beams of the *Nautilus'* beacon back at us. What a marvellous sight it was!

Suddenly, the *Nautilus* began moving at a great speed. The tranquil reflections of the ice had changed into blazing streaks which stung our eyes to look at.

Just then, we felt another blow rocking through the vessel. The *Nautilus'* spur had struck a large block of ice. Then, instead of going forward, the vessel reversed. This made me nervous, but I had to trust Captain Nemo's judgement. To distract myself, I began reading.

A little while later, a second collision took place. I grew pale with fear. Just then, Captain Nemo entered the room.

"We're stuck," he said.

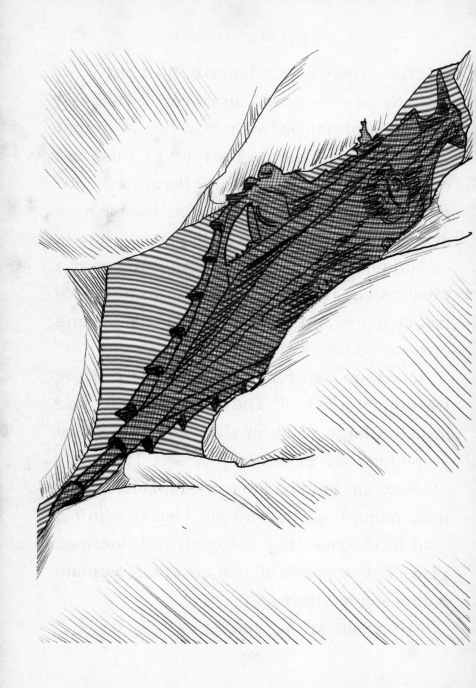

That was not the end of the bad news. "Our air reserves will be used up within forty-eight hours," said the captain. "We will try to free ourselves before then by cutting up one of the ice walls surrounding us."

Ned Land and even Captain Nemo joined the crewmen as they wore their diving suits and went outside to pick at the ice. After two hours of hard work, Ned Land returned to us, completely exhausted.

Conseil and I joined the new batch of workmen that went out to pick at the ice. At this rate, it would still take five nights and four days to complete the work.

"That's far too long!" pronounced Ned Land. "And that's without taking into account the fact that once we are free, we'll still be under the ice bank, unable to surface for water."

To add to our woes, the ice was reforming sooner than we were able to pick at it. All we could do is work faster.

When I returned on board that night, I was almost asphyxiated. Captain Nemo was forced to release a few spouts of compressed oxygen into the vessel.

It had been five days since we had gotten trapped under the ice. Even today, as I write these lines, I feel an involuntary shudder of fear wrack my body. My lungs still seem short of air!

That's when I saw Captain Nemo standing silent, as if he was thinking of an idea.

"Boiling water," he muttered.

"Boiling water?"

"Yes!" he repeated. "Boiling water! If the *Nautilus'* pumps injected streams of boiling water, it would help melt the ice!"

"It's worth a try," I said.

So try we did, and thankfully, it seemed to work. Slowly, the ice around the vessel loosened. But we were not in the clear — we had to renew our supplies of oxygen at the earliest.

I was feeling very poorly by this time. My lungs were gasping desperately for oxygen, now growing scarcer and scarcer. Hearing these words brought tears to my eyes.

Working with the oxygen tank was a relief. However, not a single man stayed a minute over their shift. They surrendered their tanks to their companions and resigned to breathing the stale air in the *Nautilus*.

When I returned from my shift, I felt half-dead with suffocation. When I woke up, I was reeling like a drunk. My companions were the same. Some crewmen were at their last gasp!

Despite the buzzing in my head, I could hear the ice cracking. The *Nautilus* began slipping downwards. I could not speak. Instead, I clutched Conseil's hand, squeezing it with involuntary convulsions.

All at once, the *Nautilus* sank into the waters like a cannonball. We were free! But how long would it be until we could surface? I would be dead first! My face was purple and my lips blue. I had lost my sight, hearing, my sense of time and even my motor skills. I was slipping into death …

Suddenly, I regained consciousness. A few whiffs of fresh oxygen had entered into my lungs. Had we managed to surface?

No! If I could breathe, it was all thanks to my gallant friends, Ned and Conseil. They had one of the oxygen tanks with them. Instead of using it themselves, they had saved it for me! I tried to push the device away, but they held down my hands.

My eyes flew towards the pressure gauge, which indicated that we were only about twenty feet from the ocean's surface. Could we break through the ice? In any case, the *Nautilus* was going to try. It attacked the ice sheet from below, like a battering ram of war. It split it little by little — backing up and then hitting it with full speed. Finally, it broke through the barrier, crushing the ice beneath its weight. The hatches were opened, sending waves of clean air into every part of the *Nautilus*.

Chapter Nineteen

Man to Beast

The three of us rushed to the platform to breathe in the fresh air. I saw that we were alone on the platform. The crewmen were content to breathe the air that entered through the hatches.

The first words I spoke were to Conseil and Ned. "My friends," I said. "We are bound to each other forever now, and I am infinitely in debt to you both."

"I will hold you to that," said the Canadian. "You will come with me when I leave this infernal *Nautilus*."

"Are we now going towards Europe?" wondered Conseil.

"Indeed we are," I replied. "We are going towards the sun, which lies north of here."

The *Nautilus* went speedily through the ocean. Before long, we had reached South American waters. To Ned's disappointment, the vessel ploughed through the ocean at a dizzying speed.

We had been on the *Nautilus* for six months and had travelled 17,000 leagues so far. We were near the Bahamas, and our path was marked by high submarine cliffs, shrouded by weeds.

"These cliffs are the perfect hiding places for giant squids," I said. "I should not be surprised to spot a few."

Sure enough, a few days later, I spotted a horrible squid outside the vessel. It was about eight yards long, swimming around the *Nautilus* while watching it with its huge green eyes. Its eight tentacles — attached to its head — were twice as long as its body. The inner surfaces were covered with hundreds of suction cups. Its mouth, large and horned like a parrot's, opened and shut vertically. But its most horrifying feature was certainly its horned tongue, complete with its own set of teeth. It probably weighed close to 25,000 kilograms.

I was so overcome by its grotesque appearance that I brought out a pencil and began to draw it. By that time, more squids had joined — I counted seven. Suddenly, the *Nautilus* stopped, trembling with shock.

"Have we hit something?" I asked.

We hadn't. The *Nautilus* was floating, but it didn't move for a whole minute. Captain Nemo and his lieutenant stepped inside. He went to the window, looked at the squids and ordered for the panels to close.

"We are going to have to fight them," said the Captain. "Man to beast. They seem to have entangled their jaws in the blades."

"That will be difficult."

"Yes," agreed Captain Nemo. "Especially since our electric bullets are powerless against them. But we shall attack with our hatchets."

"And the harpoon," said Ned Land.

We followed the Captain towards the central staircase. There, around ten men were already ready for the attack. Conseil and I took two hatchets, while Ned Land took a harpoon.

In the meanwhile, the *Nautilus* had risen to the surface. One of the crewmen unscrewed the panels, which rose up violently, apparently drawn by a squid. Immediately, its tentacles shot through the opening towards us.

With a blow of his axe, Captain Nemo chopped off the tentacle. Just then, another one appeared, lifting up one of the crewmen with great force. We all rushed out.

It was a horrible scene. The poor man was held in the air by the squid's tentacle. "Help! Help!" he cried — in French! I got a shock. I had a fellow-countryman on board, and here he was,

in this unfortunate situation. Captain Nemo rushed to the squid and with one blow of his axe, cut through a tentacle. Soon, seven of its eight arms had been cut off. Only one wriggled in the air — the one which held the crewman! Just as we threw ourselves upon it, the creature ejected a jet of black ink, blinding us. By the time our eyesight was restored, the squid had disappeared, taking the Frenchman with it.

There were ten or twelve more to deal with. Ned boldly plunged his harpoon into the eyes of the monsters. But my brave friend was suddenly tripped by a fat tentacle.

The squid opened its beak over Ned Land, nearly about to cut him in two. But Captain Nemo rushed towards it, throwing his axe into its jaws. Ned Land, with an amazing burst of energy, drove his harpoon deep into its heart.

The combat had lasted only a quarter of an hour before the defeated monsters left us. Captain Nemo, covered with blood, gazed into the sea that had swallowed his friend, his eyes glazed with tears.

That terrible incident left an indelible stain on all of us. The most affected was Captain Nemo. This was the second companion he had lost since we came on board.

The *Nautilus* suffered, too. Not seeming to want to leave the waters in which he lost his crewman, the Captain allowed his vessel to drift aimlessly upon the waves. It was only after ten days that we continued northwards.

One day, Ned came up to me. "Professor," he said. "After that ordeal in the South Pole, I do not want to follow this Nemo to the North."

"It's not practical to flee now, Ned," I replied.

"Then speak to the Captain," he said. "I would rather drown than stay here any longer!"

I decided to let the matter rest once and for all. I knocked upon the Captain's door. There was no answer. I knocked once again, and turned the handle.

Captain Nemo was bent over his work table, immersed in his work. He still hadn't seen me. So I walked towards him. He raised his head and frowned. "What do you want?" he asked roughly. "To speak to you, Captain," I replied.

"Regarding what?" he asked. "Can't you see that I am busy?"

Before I could reply, he pointed to a manuscript on his table. "This manuscript contains my life story and all my learnings from the sea," he said. "I will shut it in a waterproof case and have the last survivor of the *Nautilus* throw it into the sea."

"That is a fine idea, Captain," I said. "But isn't your idea a little old-fashioned? My companions and I would be willing to keep the manuscript, if you give us the freedom—"

"Freedom?" said the Captain, rising.

"Yes, sir," I replied. "We have been here for seven months, and we wanted to know if you intend for us to stay here forever."

217

"Whoever enters the *Nautilus* must never quit it," said the Captain. "If you feel otherwise, I cannot help you. That is the end of that."

I related this conversation to my friends. Instead of being discouraged, Ned's resolve became even stronger. But even though he was planning escape, nature, it seemed, did not wish to connive with him. We were plagued with stormy weather while we sailed near the coast of North America.

Upset at missing his chance while so close to home, Ned grew even surlier and distant. In the meanwhile, by the end of May, the *Nautilus* had arrived near the coast of Ireland, before turning to the south—towards Europe.

Then, on May 31, the *Nautilus* did an odd thing—it circled around the same area all day, as if looking for some specific spot. This continued until the next day. Captain Nemo appeared on the platform to take some measurements. Then, he announced, "It is here."

They were going to close the hatches, so I went downstairs and watched the *Nautilus* sink to the ocean bed. There, I saw a huge shipwreck through the panels. It had probably been there for several years.

Just then, I heard Captain Nemo walk up to me. He said: "This ship was once called the *Marseillais*. But after several brave battles that it undertook, the French changed its name. On this very day, seventy-four years ago, this ship fought heroically with an enemy English vessel. After losing three masts, with water in its hold and a third of its crew injured, it preferred to sink than surrender.

They nailed their flag to the poop, and the ship sunk with all its 356 sailors crying "Long live the Republic! Long live France!"

"It's the *Avenger*!" I exclaimed.

"Yes, the *Avenger*," said the captain. "What a fine name!"

Chapter Twenty

A Massacre

I was very moved by the incident with the *Avenger*. I may not know where Captain Nemo came from or where he was going, but I knew one thing — he had come to the sea not because he generally disliked people, but because of a deep-rooted hatred which time could not soften.

The sound of a dull boom brought me back from my musings.

"I went up to the platform where Conseil and Ned were already standing. "Gunshot," said Ned, before I could ask.

I looked in the direction of a vessel in the distance. It was coming towards us speedily.

"What is that ship?" I asked Ned.

"She bears no country's flag, but I bet she is a war ship," he replied. "I hope she reaches us and sinks this cursed *Nautilus*."

It was difficult to believe that the ship could see us from that distance, let alone be aware of what kind of object we were. Yet, the ship came closer in our direction. Maybe this ship could be our chance at freedom. A white smoke burst from the front of the vessel, and a few seconds later, a loud explosion struck my ear.

"They're firing at us!" I exclaimed. "Surely they can see us on the platform?"

"Maybe they are firing for that very reason," replied the Canadian. He took out his handkerchief and waved it in the air. But he had scarcely raised it when a strong arm struck him down, sending him crashing to the floor.

It was Captain Nemo. "Fool!" he shouted. "Do you want to be nailed to the *Nautilus'* spur before I drive it into this infernal vessel?"

The Captain was terrible to hear and even more terrible to look at. His face was pale, his pupils contracted and his breath ragged. He turned away from the Canadian and towards the war ship.

"Oh, you ship of a wretched nation!" he screamed. "You know who I am! I do not need to see your colours to recognise you! Look! And I will show you mine!"

He unfurled a black flag similar to the one he had placed at the South Pole. At that moment, a shot struck the hull of the *Nautilus* and bounced off into the sea.

"Go down!" he told me. "And take your companions with you!"

"Captain!" I cried. "Are you going to attack the vessel?"

"I'm going to sink it!" he replied.

"You can't do that!" I said.

"I will do that," replied the Captain coldly. "And you will not judge me for it! Fate has

shown you things you ought not to have seen. Go down."

I could do nothing but obey. Around fifteen crewmen surrounded the Captain, looking angrily at the war ship. As I walked down, I heard another shot. Captain Nemo was shouting at them angrily.

I remained in my cabin, but at about four in the afternoon, I was no longer able to contain my curiosity. I walked up the central staircase to see Captain Nemo still pacing on the platform. He was looking towards the ship, which was five or six miles away. The captain broke out into a passionate speech:

"I am the law! I am the judge!" he exclaimed. "I am the oppressed and they are the oppressor! Because of them, I have lost everything that I loved and cherished — my country, my wife, my children, my parents — I saw them all perish!"

I re-joined my friends downstairs. "Let us flee," I said.

"I agree," said Ned Land. "Let's wait for the right opportunity."

We made a plan to flee when the war ship was nearby. We could try to save them from the cruel fate that awaited them. But Captain Nemo did not allow them to come nearby.

The next day, at 5 o'clock, I saw that the *Nautilus* was going slower. "My friends," I said, "the moment has arrived. "

We passed through the library, but just as I pushed open the door to the central staircase, the *Nautilus* began to sink. I understood Captain Nemo's plan of attack—he was going to strike the ship from underneath.

Once again, we were prisoners. We took refuge in my cabin and sat without speaking. I felt *Nautilus* charge forward. The steel spur was hacking away at the war ship like a needle through sailcloth.

I rushed outside, only to see Captain Nemo seated in the room, looking as gloomy as ever.

Through the panels, I could see the large ship, wrecked. All around, I could see humans holding onto stray planks of wood for dear life.

When the ship had completely sunk, Captain Nemo walked into his room. My eyes followed him inside, and on the wall beneath his heroes, I spotted the portrait of a woman with two young children. Captain Nemo looked at the portrait and stretched his arms towards it. Then, he fell to his knees, breaking out into deep sobs.

In the coming days, Captain Nemo was never to be seen. The *Nautilus* always seemed to be submerged. On the few occasions when it resurfaced, the hatches opened and shut mechanically. Ned had gotten so surly and depressed, that Conseil, afraid that he might try to take his own life, watched him constantly.

One morning, I was shaken awake by Ned Land. "It is time," he was saying in a low voice. "Will you be ready tonight?"

"Yes," I said. "We will flee tonight."

I had decided to leave the *Nautilus*. I spent the whole day in a nervous tizzy. I was not hungry, but I ate a small dinner at half-past six. Just as I had finished, Ned Land came to my cabin.

"We leave at ten," he said. "Conseil and I will wait for you in the boat."

I dressed myself in warm clothes and bundled up my notes. What was Captain Nemo doing? I put my ear at his door. I heard footsteps — he was still awake.

In my mind's eye, I relived my journey, every incident which had occurred on board the *Nautilus*. Thinking about these made Captain Nemo seemed like a legend of the sea.

At half-past nine, I heard the strains of the piano from outside — a sad, soulful harmony. I listened with my whole being.

That's when I realised that I would have to pass by Captain Nemo on my way to the longboat. He would see me; perhaps he would even speak to me.

Soon, the moment had come for me to move. I opened my door and crept along the stairs of the *Nautilus*. When I reached the door of the saloon, I opened it gingerly. It was completely dark. Captain Nemo was there, but he did not notice me. I walked through the room silently.

Just as I was about to open the door at the opposite side, Captain Nemo sighed. I could hear him rising up. He came towards me, gliding like a ghost, his breast shaking with silent sobs. I heard him murmur these words:

"Almighty God! Enough! Enough!"

In desperation, I rushed away, mounted the central stairway, made my way up the upper flight and reached the longboat. My friends were already there, waiting for me.

As we unfastened the boat from the vessel, I heard the sound of loud voices coming from the ship. Had they discovered our escape?

We heard one word repeated over and over again. And then we realised — it was not us that the crew was worried about!

"The maelstrom! The maelstrom!" they said. The maelstrom was a ferocious whirlpool that could capture even the strongest vessel. The *Nautilus* had been driven into this deadly pit.

As the longboat was still attached to the main vessel, we began to fall into the spiral whirlpool ourselves. "Hold on!" shouted Ned, "And look after the bolts! We might be saved if we stick to the *Nautilus*!"

But he had barely completed his sentence when we heard the bolts give way with a crash. The longboat was hurled like a stone into the middle of the whirlpool.

My head struck a piece of iron, and I lost all consciousness.

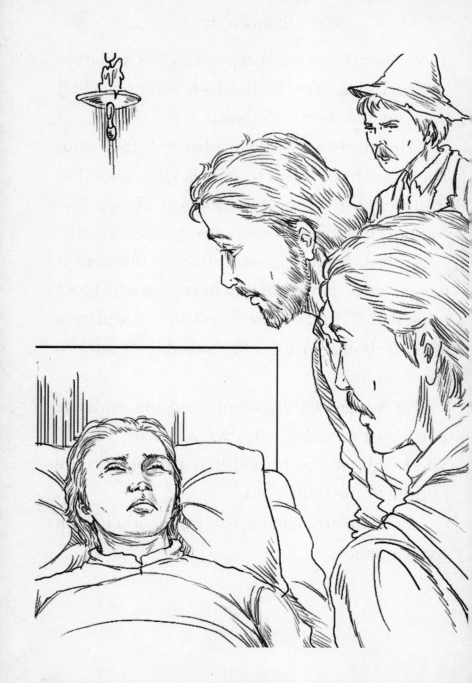

Chapter Twenty-One

Conclusion

I had no idea how our boat escaped from the maelstrom, or how Ned, Conseil and myself emerged from it.

When I returned to consciousness, I found myself in a fisherman's hut on the Loffoden Isles with my two faithful companions.

We could not return to France immediately, as the steamboat appeared only once a month. It is in this fine place that I write an account of my adventures.

Will people believe me? I don't know. It does not matter much anyway. All I know is that I have earned the right to speak of the ocean,

under which, in less than ten months, I have crossed 20,000 leagues.

What happened to the *Nautilus*? Did it survive the maelstrom? Is Captain Nemo still alive? Does he still sail the oceans, or did he retire after that great misfortune?

Will the waves carry his manuscript one day? Shall I ever know his real name? Will I learn his nationality?

I certainly hope so. I also hope that the *Nautilus* overcame the maelstrom, and that Captain Nemo still travels the ocean — his adopted country — upon it. May his wondrous tours of the ocean extinguish his thirst for revenge! May the judge inside him disappear, leaving only the philosopher to peacefully continue exploring the sea!

In the Bible, the book of Ecclesiastes asks, "Have you walked in search of the soundless depths?" Two men in all of humanity have earned the right to answer this question: Captain Nemo and myself.

About the Author

Jules Verne was born on February 8, 1828, in the harbour city of Nantes, France. Seeing the ships come and go inspired Verne to write captivating tales of travel and adventure.

After studying law, Verne found himself attracted to theatre and opera. Thus, he started his writing career with short plays and operas. To supplement his income, he began working as a stockbroker, but still continued to write. His hard work bore fruit at the age of thirty-five, when his novel, *Five Weeks in a Balloon* (1863), was published to wide acclaim.

Many of his works have gone down in history as classic works of literature. Some of these include *Journey to the Centre of the Earth* (1864), *Twenty Thousand Leagues Under the Sea* (1870) and *Around the World in Eighty Days* (1873).

Jules Verne died on March 24, 1905 in his home in Amiens, France, leaving behind a great legacy. Today, he is the second-most translated author in the world. Because of his futuristic novels that described technology that was only invented years later, he is often referred to as 'The Father of Science Fiction'.

■ Characters

Professor Pierre Arronax: The narrator of the story, Professor Arronax is forty years old at the beginning of the story. He lives in Paris with his manservant, Conseil. He joins the expedition on the *Abraham Lincoln* as a subject expert and a representative of France.

Conseil: Professor Arronax's servant. Conseil is thirty years old at the beginning of the story. He is extremely faithful to his master,

238

and always refers to him in the third person. He enjoys memorising biological classifications of animals.

Ned Land: A talented Canadian harpooner travelling upon the *Abraham Lincoln*. He is forty years old at the beginning of the story. He is stubborn, quiet, impatient and short-tempered.

Captain Nemo: The mysterious commander of the *Nautilus*. He is very passionate and emotional, but considers himself estranged from society. He is very rich and very brilliant, having masterminded, designed and built the *Nautilus* himself.

Commander Farragut: The commander of the *Abraham Lincoln*.

■ Questions

Chapter One
- *Describe the animal that Professor Arronax believed the sea monster was.*
- *What did Conseil mean by "I think we will be as comfortable a hermit crab in the shell of a whelk!"?*

Chapter Two
- *Which member of the crew spotted the narwhal first?*

Chapter Three
- *Why was the Abraham Lincoln fleeing instead of fighting?*

Chapter Four
- *How did Conseil and Professor Arronax stay afloat?*

Chapter Five
- *Why did Professor Arronax wake up feeling short of breath?*

Chapter Six
- *What did Captain Nemo say that convinced Professor Arronax to accept his offer?*

Chapter Seven
- *How did Captain Nemo manage to build the Nautilus in secret?*

Chapter Eight
- *Describe the diving equipment found in the Nautilus.*

Chapter Nine
- *What was the name of the sinking ship?*

Chapter Ten
- *How did Captain Nemo plan to free the Nautilus from the reef?*
- *Who was most keen to go hunting on the island?*

Chapter Eleven
- *Describe the coral graveyard.*

Chapter Twelve
- *Near which island did they go pearl diving?*

Chapter Thirteen
- *Describe the animal that Ned Land hunted.*

Chapter Fourteen
- *Describe the strange incident with the diver.*

Chapter Fifteen
- *What did Captain Nemo do with the sunken treasures he found?*

Chapter Sixteen
- *What do you know about the lost continent of Atlantis?*

Chapter Seventeen
- *Why was the Nautilus shaking violently?*

Chapter Eighteen
- *Why did Captain Nemo agree to hunt the sperm whales, but not the baleen whales?*

Chapter Nineteen
- *Recount the story of the Avenger.*

Chapter Twenty
- *Why was the war ship attacking the Nautilus?*

Chapter Twenty-One
- *Where did Professor Arronax find himself when he woke up?*